Dear Readers,

We're so thrilled to finally be able to [...]
that has been several years in the mak[...]

We've been friends for nearly two de[...]
of each other's writing. Over the years, our conversations have often
turned to the topic of what our series characters, Jack Reacher and Will
Trent, would do if they met in real life. Would Will arrest Reacher for
taking out some vigilante justice on a bad guy? Would Reacher break
Will's face or throw him down a well? The challenge was finding a way
for them to work together. Both men have strong moral compasses,
but they each reach true north in very different ways. Finding a
case that would bring them into each other's orbit was a very long
conversation that finally resulted in a plot that we were both excited
to work out on the page.

The result is *Cleaning the Gold*. We started off writing our own
chapters separately, but as the stories became intertwined, things
merged, so you won't necessarily know who wrote what—and we really
hope you enjoy it. No matter what, we think Jack and Will had a pretty
good time navigating the beginning of a beautiful friendship …

Best wishes,

CLEANING THE GOLD

Also by Karin Slaughter

Also by Lee Child

CLEANING THE GOLD

A JACK REACHER AND WILL TRENT SHORT STORY

KARIN SLAUGHTER

LEE CHILD

WILLIAM MORROW

An Imprint of HarperCollinsPublishers

Lyrics from:
"Africa" by David F. Paich and Jeffrey T. Porcaro
"I'm on Fire" by Bruce Springsteen

CLEANING THE GOLD. Copyright © 2019 by Karin Slaughter and Lee Child.

Excerpt from *The Last Widow* © 2019 by Karin Slaughter.

Excerpt from *Blue Moon* by Lee Child © 2019 by Lee Child.

Will Trent is a trademark of Karin Slaughter Publishing LLC.

HarperCollins books may be purchased for educational, business, or sales promotional use. For information, please email the Special Markets Department at SPsales@harpercollins.com.

An electronic edition of this book was published in 2019 by William Morrow.

FIRST WILLIAM MORROW PAPERBACK EDITION PUBLISHED 2020.

Designed by Diahann Sturge

Library of Congress Cataloging-in-Publication Data has been applied for.

ISBN 978-0-06-297830-1

23 24 25 26 27 LBC 11 10 9 8 7

CLEANING THE GOLD

1

Will Trent sat across from a closed office door listening to mumbled voices discussing the two DUIs and spotty work history on his employment application. The conversation did not seem to be going in his favor. Not good. Will needed this job. Otherwise his real job was screwed.

He wiped his forehead with his sleeve. The temperature outside had already passed the boiling point. Inside was not much better. His sweat had started to sweat in the dank, 1950s tomb of a government building. The low ceiling sagged even lower. The drywall was swollen from humidity. He watched a bead of perspiration drop from his nose and roll across the floor. A gutter ran down the middle of the linoleum from decades of Army boots trotting up and down the hallway.

Will shifted in the chair. His vertebrae had transformed into zip ties strangling his spinal column. The muscles in his legs were congealing. His body ached for two reasons. The first was from the send-off his girlfriend had given him the night before. And this morning at the aptly named park and ride. The second was because he'd spent the entire one-hour flight from Atlanta to Lexington with his knees punching into the seat in front of him, jammed between a toddler screaming at a paperclip and a flatulent senior citizen.

Only one of those reasons was worth the ache.

From behind the door, a voice bellowed, "I don't give a good God damn what you think, Dave."

Colonel Stephanie Lukather, the woman in charge of the United States Bullion Depository. An important command, but what did Will know? Most of his knowledge of the federal government's gold reserves came courtesy of Wikipedia and *Goldfinger*.

The facility was adjacent to the Fort Knox Army base, located at the intersection of Bullion Boulevard and Gold Vault Road. The main door was twenty tons of drill- and torch-resistant material measuring twenty-one inches thick. Around $350 billion in precious metals was stored inside. The US Mint Police guarded the facility and the US Army guarded them. The vault had been opened for public inspection just once, in September of 1974. Previously, in 1964, Pussy Galore had knocked out the entire base with her Flying Circus and a dirty bomb inside the vault had been disarmed with 0.07 seconds to spare.

The door finally swung open.

Major Dave Baldani gave Will a smirky look.

Will knew that look. It was the way a good guy put a bad guy in his place. He used it a lot in his day job as a special agent with the Georgia Bureau of Investigation. But Will wasn't at Fort Knox as a cop. He was working undercover as an ex-Army captain who'd fallen down the rabbit hole of stupid decisions after two tours of duty in Afghanistan.

His ID was air-tight unless you could crack the Pentagon's database. Jack Phineas Wolfe, honorably discharged in 2016. Two DUIs. Community service. Probation. Divorced. No kids. Overdrawn at the bank. Maxed out on his credit cards. Evicted from his last known place of residence. Car repo'd by the bank. Searching for honest work, or as close to honest as he could get.

"Hurry, boys." Colonel Lukather was early fifties, lean and trim with her long blonde hair pinned up in a military style. She gave an impatient roll of her hand. "I'm waiting for you."

Will had to duck his head to stand. The drop-ceiling was eighteen inches lower than it should've been. The dark paneled walls had buckled with age. Locked filing cabinets lined one side of the room. The colonel's regulation metal desk was shoved against the other side. There were no windows. The air didn't move. He could've been standing inside of a coffin.

Colonel Lukather pointed up at the low ceiling, explaining, "Brig Gen upstairs wanted a shower in his office. Shit rolls downhill. I don't need a skylight, Wolfe. Sit."

Will took one of the chairs across from her. Baldani

remained standing about two inches from Will's shoulder—another good guy/bad guy trick.

Lukather said, "Wolfe, you've been in some trouble since you FTA'd."

Will didn't hear a question, so he didn't give an answer.

Lukather rested her hand on his file, waiting for the ensuing silence to wear him down.

Will didn't wear.

The clock on the wall gave a sharp *tock*.

Baldani let out a long, smoker's wheeze of a sigh.

"Dave, looks like we've got ourselves a genuine Captain Jack here." Lukather opened the file and pretended to read the information for the first time. "Stationed in BFE. Fifth in your class at John Wayne School. Stacked up your chest candy in the Sandbox. Earned your Triple Threat. Quite the gung-ho mo-fo. You certainly win the big dick contest in the room."

Will hadn't had time to study any Army jargon, so he was clueless except for the last bit, which seemed accurate.

"Then—" A page was turned in the file. Lukather's finger trailed down Jack Wolfe's background check. "Two DUIs. Bad divorce. Bad credit. What makes you think I should pay you fifteen dollars an hour and put you up in one of my hotels for the privilege of working on my base for the next few days?"

Will shrugged with one shoulder in the same eat-shit way perps did when he was interrogating them. "Up to you."

Baldani shifted on his feet, clearly annoyed.

Lukather looked up from the paperwork. Maybe she gave Will credit for honesty, because she didn't tell him to get the hell out of her office. "Do you know what the job is?"

"Janitorial?" Will shrugged again, solely to piss off Baldani. "The posting mentioned something about cleaning."

She said, "Not your usual butts and elbows. What do you know about gold?"

Another shrug. "I could use some."

"All right, shitbrain." Baldani had reached his limit. "Check the attitude. You're talking to a full bird colonel."

Will turned his chin two degrees, ignoring him, but not ignoring him.

Baldani's fists clenched, which was stupid because the minute he raised his arms, Will could punch the guy's nutsac into his asshole.

"That's enough, boys." Lukather closed Jack Wolfe's file. The employment decision had been made, but she didn't choose to share it. Instead, she told Will, "Gold is a naturally occurring chemical element with the atomic number 79. It is classed as a soft metal, so it can easily be scratched or damaged. The oil on your hands can corrode or tarnish the finish, diminishing the value. When handling, it's recommended that you wear lint-free, cotton gloves. Masks are required because the moisture from your breath or saliva can leave spots that can't be removed."

Will waited for the rest of the speech.

"Executive Order 6102, issued by President Franklin D. Roosevelt in 1933, outlawed the private ownership of gold coins, bullion and gold certificates, which forced citizens to sell those items to the Federal Reserve. In 1936, the Treasury Department began construction of the Gold Vault, eventually transferring via a heavily armored train convoy the majority of the gold reserves to our facility. We currently have deep-stored in sealed vaults north of 147.3 million troy ounces, primarily in the form of 12.4-kilogram gold bars that range from .900 to .999 purity. The rest of the nation's reserve is held by West Point and Denver."

Will raised his eat-shit shoulder again. "And?"

"By order of Congress, the vaults are examined annually by the Treasury Department's Office of the Inspector General. Eyeballs only. It would take months to check the serial numbers of each individual gold bar against the inventory. Which is what brings us to the here and now, Captain Wolfe. TS/Ultra 42–12 under the 1978 Compartmentalization of Treasury's Governing Acts requires that each item of gold be manually inspected every ten years. We are at our current ten-year mark in that process, and we find ourselves with days to go and one man down."

Will retired the shoulder shrug. He rubbed his jaw, trying to tamp down the invisible teenage Will that was jumping around like a meth-head on a pogo stick. He had hoped that the undercover job could take him inside the facility, but this was inside the vaults. With the gold. They were talking Oddjob territory.

He had to get clarification. "You want me to handle the gold?"

"You're basically a maid," Baldani said. "You clean the gold. That's what the Act really stands for. CTG. Cleaning the gold."

Lukather supplied, "It takes us exactly nine months to get through the full inventory, and I happen to be ahead of schedule right now, which is a very good thing. We work twenty-four-seven, with two teams of six in the daylight hours, two more teams of six from balls to eight. For security reasons, no team gets more than two weeks inside the vaults, and we use outside personnel— preferably former Army—so no one on base gets too familiar with the comings and goings. As I said, we're damn close to the finish line, but day shift needs another cog in the machine."

Will considered her words. She hadn't actually offered him the job, but she'd read him into an ultra-top-secret program, which was as good as. Now would not be the time to appear too eager. "What does it take?"

"Hard work," Baldani said, managing to convey with his snarly tone that he doubted Will had it in him.

Lukather said, "Dave's not wrong. The glamor wears off in half an hour. From then on, it's back-breaking work. You're obviously still in fighting shape, Wolfe.

Lost your yut-cut, but I still see the soldier in you." She sat back in her chair, openly appraising him. "What're you, six-four, two-ten?"

Will had been one-eighty-five since high school, but he nodded.

"Dave thinks you're trouble, but I like a little bit of trouble." She grinned openly at Will. "Besides, the last guy Dave recommended bugged out when he broke his first sweat. Are you that kind of pussy, Captain?"

Will shook his head. "I don't have a lot of quit in me."

"I bet you don't." She winked away something in her eye. "I like having a hard-working man underneath me. Are you a hard, working man, Wolfe?"

Will wasn't a stranger to manual labor. "I get the job done."

"I bet you do, soldier." She gave a deep, throaty laugh. "Baldani, slot him in. Hooah."

Baldani looked like he wanted to argue, but Lukather looked like the kind of woman you couldn't argue with, and not just because of the birds on her shoulders.

Baldani grumbled, "Let's go, asswipe."

The asswipe earned Baldani the pleasure of watching Will take his time getting out of the chair. To rub it in, he made a show of ducking under the low ceiling, mostly because Baldani had a foot of clearance. The major looked up at Will with a specific kind of fury in his eyes. Small Man's Hysteria, Will's girlfriend called it, and she should know because she was taller than Baldani, too.

In the hallway, the major didn't walk so much as toss

his boots out in front of him. He was fit for a tubby guy, probably spending equal amounts of time at the bar and the gym. His hair was cut Beetle Bailey tight to his head, which didn't do a lot to hide the bald spot at the crown. Baldani caught Will's eyes on the sunburned patch of scalp. He covered it with his hand, pretending to wipe away sweat. He threw a look at Will, then threw it again when Will chuckled.

"Don't think for a second Lukather's sweet on you," Baldani warned. "She'd sit on a door knob if it pinched her nipple."

Will decided to really fuck with the guy. "Who wouldn't?"

Outside, the sun sliced into his face like a razor. Will could hear gunfire in the distance. Then an explosion. Then more gunfire, which really made him wish he had a gun and/or something to blow up.

There was a reason Will was a cop.

Baldani climbed into a blue Impala with mud stalactites hanging from the undercarriage. The air conditioning was set on stun by the time Will got in. He experienced that familiar sensation of sweat dripping down his back while his nose ran from the cold. Baldani swung the car around. The radio was already up loud, but Baldani twisted the knob higher because nothing proved you were a badass like blowing out a subwoofer with "Smells Like Teen Spirit."

Will summoned his Wikipedia knowledge as the car squealed out of the parking lot. The post sprawled over

100,000 acres spanning three different counties. Nearly 13,000 people lived here with thousands more rotating in for training or support. There were hotels and fast-food restaurants and mini-malls and a bowling alley and a medical complex and family housing and K-12 schools. For every 100 females over the age of eighteen, there were 190.3 males, which might explain why Baldani was wound so tight.

Or maybe the guy was just a dick.

Off the main road, Will spotted more office buildings than he could count. The Army's Human Resources Command called the base home, which Will gathered meant this was where paperwork came to die. Still, he was on an active Army base with a high level of security. Just getting past the main gate had taken two hours of waiting and a great deal of sweating over his various forms of Jack Phineas Wolfe fake-but-not-fake government-issued IDs.

The Gold Vault came into view at the end of a long road. The white granite building was fairly innocuous-looking, a typical art deco structure from the 1930s, the kind of thing that was more beautiful than it should've been because the Great Depression had put a chunk of the country out of work and people took their time making things when they had the luxury of a living wage.

Will had seen the vault from the highway and thought his eyes were playing tricks on him. It didn't seem right that something like that was out in the open. Then he'd clocked the razor wire and rows of electric fences and warning signs and Jeeps zigzagging around what was probably ten football fields' worth of claymore mines. There were no snipers on the roof, but by the time a would-be thief made his way across the wide-open fields surrounding the structure, there could be at least two hundred men aiming down on him.

Baldani pulled to a stop beside a low, one-story security building just inside the open gates. Though *open* was misleading. The heavy iron gates were swung back, but twelve bollards stuck up from the pavement. Rows of tire spikes jutted into the air like crocodile teeth.

Baldani told Will, "Time to bend over and cough, Wolfie."

The car door was opened by a guard who looked like bags of Sakrete had been packed inside of his shirt. Will looked around, shielding his eyes from the sun. The last time he'd been surrounded by this many heavily-armed men, he was raiding a warehouse at the Port of Savannah under a joint operation with the FBI, DEA and ATF.

Baldani tossed his keys, cigarette lighter and ID onto a tray that was put through an X-ray machine, but that was the end of his examination. He leaned against the fence and lit a cigarette as he waited for Will to be processed. Getting on to the base had been difficult, but the scrutiny at the vault was like . . . getting into Fort Knox.

Will counted ten guards with M4s slung around their necks, the big-boy upgrade to the civilian AR-15. Their belts completed the look with Sig Sauer P-320s, pepper spray, Tasers and telescoping metal batons. They moved quickly, efficiently, pushing and pulling Will down a conveyor belt of scrutiny. A burly German Shepherd shoved his nose into Will's crotch. A teenager with a laptop raided Will's wallet and scanned various fake IDs into the system. Will's boots were put through the X-ray machine. He had to take off his belt and hold up his arms as a wand checked him for metal, then he was still patted down and asked to show his Chapstick and keys. Then a second guy patted him down again. Then a third ran a small piece of paper over Will's hands and stuck it into a machine to check for bomb-making residue.

The Impala was getting a similar once-over. Another guard ran a mirror underneath the car, knocking off the stalactites. A Belgian Shepherd was given free rein. Seats were pulled up. Floor mats and visors were flipped. The glove box was opened. The engine and trunk were checked. Someone ran a Geiger counter around the periphery. Someone else checked for explosive residue.

Will was already sweating from the heat, but a kind of flop-sweat dripped from his scalp when he was told to give a fingerprint scan. Would his Jack Phineas Wolfe cover hold up to this level of interrogation, or would Will end up getting shot where he stood?

Now was not the best time to be asking this question.

None of the guards looked old enough to legally buy alcohol. One of them still had peach fuzz on his chin. Another could've passed for Groot going through puberty. They all had the same bored look in their eyes that could easily lead to a trigger being pulled, a baton being slung, and Will being airlifted to the hospital or driven to the morgue.

His heart jackknifed against his ribs when the teenager with the laptop stepped back into Will's personal space. The kid had Jack Wolfe's driver's license, VA health insurance card, social security card and, for some reason, his Costco card.

"Look into this." Another guard was holding up a pair of heavy, black goggles. A springy cord ran from the top and plugged into a tablet.

Will pressed his face into the goggles. He saw nothing but black, then a line crossed his vision that gave him the sensation of eyeballing a Cylon from *Battlestar Galactica*.

The sun blinded him when the goggles were pulled away.

"Retina scan," Baldani offered. The half-smoked cigarette dangled from his lips. He looked like he was enjoying Will's discomfort which, fair enough, was exactly what Will would've been doing in his place.

"Sir?" The kid with the laptop was back up in Will's business. He was looking at Will's IDs, then looking at Will, then looking at the IDs. His laptop made a beeping sound, but he kept his eyes on Will. Will stared back. He watched sweat roll down the side of the kid's shaved head. The soldier was eighteen if he was a day, his body cut the way you were cut if every second of your free time was spent either working out or trying to get laid.

The laptop beeped again, but the kid did not look at the screen.

Will broke first. He looked down at the screen. He looked back at the kid. He looked down at the screen.

The kid yelled, "Alpha! Mike! Foxtrot!"

Will waited to get shot in the face or shoved face-down onto the asphalt.

Baldani smirked as he flicked away his cigarette. "Adios. Mother. Fucker."

The bollards dropped. The spikes were drawn back. The ten guards peeled away. Will took the deepest, most cleansing breath of his life.

Baldani smugly flashed a row of nicotine-stained Chiclet teeth as he drove up to the building. Will let him have the win, pushing the humiliation aside and turning his mind toward the job at hand. He wasn't here to beat the shit out of Dave Baldani or to clean gold bars. He was here to find a cop killer.

The initial crime had been committed on April 16, 1997, in a city one hundred miles south of Atlanta called Margrave, Georgia.

These were the facts:

A stranger was reported loitering in and around the library. Margrave was a small town. They didn't get strange people, at least not ones they didn't recognize. The loiterer was a white male with blond hair and blue eyes, well over six feet tall, built like a linebacker and dressed in dirty jeans and an Army camo jacket. Last seen pacing back and forth outside the library doors. He'd been inside once to use the bathroom and page through a copy of *A Guide to Birds of the Southeastern United States*. The librarian had called the sheriff's office when she'd heard the stranger mumbling to himself. Within five minutes, a deputy had rolled up to the scene. According to an eyewitness, the stranger had pulled out a revolver and shot the deputy in the head.

The deputy's name was Phillip Michael Deacon. Thirty-nine years old, twenty-one years on the force, a wife and teenage boy at home, a married daughter with his first grandchild on the way.

The stranger had given Deacon no warning. There were no words between the two men. Just a double-tap on the trigger, then the stranger had darted into the woods, never to be seen again.

Deacon had survived the gunshots, but it was hard to argue that he had lived. He never woke from surgery. He'd spent the next twenty-two years in a coma. Two months ago, he had finally succumbed to pneumonia, which converted the arrest warrant from attempted murder of a peace officer to murder in the first degree with aggravating circumstances, which carried the maximum penalty of death.

That was when Will's boss had dropped the file on his desk.

Will was not a fan of killers, but cop killers belonged in the Devil's favorite part of hell. He had spent every waking hour since the file had landed on his desk tracking back through the original case, even driving up to the GBI's secure warehouse in Dry Branch to search in deep storage for the only pieces of physical evidence that remained in the case, fragments from the two slugs taken out of Phillip Deacon's brain and a sealed plastic bag containing the Margrave library's copy of *A Guide to Birds of the Southeastern United States*.

There was no gun to match the fragments to.

The only identifiable fingerprints found on the book belonged to the librarian who, the morning of the shooting, had taken it brand-spanking-new out of the shipping box and placed it on the shelf.

The general public always thought of cold cases as impossible to solve. They weren't completely wrong, but oftentimes, Will found that the passage of time gave witnesses more perspective. Mostly, it came down to the simple fact that they weren't scared anymore. The bullies and thugs who'd intimidated them had either died young or ended up in prison. Marriages dissolved. Love ran out. Reputations were damaged or rebuilt. In short, a long stretch of time could lend more focus to past events.

Will had driven to the Florida panhandle and talked to the now-retired librarian who'd made the 9–1–1 call. He had tracked down the widow of the eyewitness to the shooting. He had talked to some of Deacon's fellow deputies and various patrons of the library. He had sat in countless living rooms sipping countless glasses of iced tea and listened to countless old ladies doling out the tiny pieces of information that would eventually help Will put together the puzzle.

First piece: One month after the attempted murder of Deputy Deacon outside of the library, a second stranger had shown up in Margrave.

Second piece: Stranger 2 was reportedly a white male. Blond hair. Blue eyes. Mid-thirties. Around six-foot-five and two hundred fifty pounds. Built like a linebacker, some said.

Third piece: Stranger 2 was immediately arrested for murder—not the library attempted-murder, but murder in the first of an unidentified male—by the Margrave sheriff, who also provided the only eyewitness testimony to the alleged murder. The *alleged* was thrown in there because Will could find no report or file that contained any mention of a murder during that time period.

Fourth piece: There was a prison transport record showing Stranger 2 en route to the Warburton penitentiary, but there was no record of him remaining there longer than two days.

Fifth piece: Instead of the sheriff calling in the Marshals Service and conducting a full-on manhunt for the presumed fugitive, the *alleged* murder charge was dropped, and Stranger 2 was allowed to disappear.

Until now.

"Last stop, ladies' lingerie." Baldani angled the car across two spaces like he was parking a Lamborghini instead of a government-issued Chevy.

Will heard the click of a cigarette lighter as he got

out of the car. He looked up at the imposing building. He saw guard towers, security cameras, slitted windows with rifles poking out, vast light arrays that could probably be seen from the surface of the moon.

The place was guarded like Fort Knox.

Baldani walked toward a side door, smoke trailing behind him. Will tried to keep downwind, wondering which would get Baldani first—lung cancer or skin cancer.

Not his problem.

Will ran his hand along the cool granite side of the building. He focused his mind on the heart of the case. Phillip Michael Deacon had never held his first grandchild. He had never watched his son play ball. He had never kissed his wife again or driven his car to the store or taken out the trash or scratched his own ass when it was itching because he'd rolled up on a loitering call and lost every meaningful part of his life.

Here was what Will knew about the Margrave sheriff: he was a corrupt son of a bitch.

And also very dead.

The sheriff's widow hadn't kept any of his files. His kids couldn't bear to say their father's name. The sheriff's initial eyewitness report to the *alleged* first-degree murder no longer existed. None of his former deputies would give up their boss, even as the man rotted in the ground. There had been no computers in the sheriff's office back in 1997. The only reason Will had any details on Stranger 1 was because the GBI had been called in immediately after the shooting. By order of the state legislature, the agency was in charge of investigating all officer-involved shootings.

The scant information Will had on Stranger 2 had been knotted together with strings of gossip that had eventually led him to a dusty old filing cabinet in the basement of Warburton penitentiary. The triplicate prisoner transport request on Stranger 2 had provided the requisite bullet points: The inmate's name, birthdate, physical details and mug shot. The charges filed. The sheriff's signature on the summary report that listed himself as an eyewitness.

It was some kind of crazy bad luck that Stranger 2 had arrived in Margrave, and within an hour managed to *allegedly* murder a guy in cold blood in front of only one witness, who happened to be a seasoned county sheriff.

Puzzle piece number six was a corner piece: During the period of time between Phillip Michael Deacon getting shot and Stranger 2's arrest, Will had found no proof of any murders in the tri-county area. No newspaper reports. No local gossip. No funeral home records. No death certificate registered with Georgia's Division of Public Health and Vital Records.

The only thing that made sense to Will was that the crooked sheriff had framed Stranger 2 for a murder that did not happen.

Which—why?

The most likely answer to this question helped Will

see the picture that the individual pieces had started to form: Stranger 1 had to be Stranger 2, because—

Seven: The two strangers' physical descriptions were identical.

Eight: Both strangers had coincidentally shown up in a Podunk town that never saw strangers.

Nine, another corner: Will had emailed the now-retired librarian in Florida a scan of the mug shot from Stranger 2's prison transport file. She had written back immediately, stating with absolute certainty that Stranger 2 was Stranger 1, the man she had reported for loitering back in 1997. The man that an eyewitness had identified as the man who had shot Phillip Michael Deacon twice in the head.

Ergo, Will had his man.

"Thissaway, Wolfe." Baldani took one last hit on his cigarette before he opened the door.

The air inside the building was at least ten degrees cooler. Will followed Baldani down a steep flight of stairs. They hit the landing at a locked steel door, then walked up another flight of stairs. Then down again. Will was thinking this was another one of Baldani's pranks, but then they entered a large hall with polished white marble gleaming from every surface.

All of the sweat on Will's body turned to ice.

The room felt like money. Not tech money or hedge fund money, but real-deal J. D. Rockefeller "Puttin' on the Ritz" money. The ceiling was decorated in gold leaf. The mahogany benches had intricate designs hand-carved into the backs. Museum-level artwork hung on the walls. Will walked up to one of the glass display cases.

"Some kind of old book," Baldani provided.

"Gutenberg Bible." Will had never been to church, but he felt like he should whisper the words.

"Yeah," Baldani said. "They kept a copy of the Magna Carta here during WWII. The original US Constitution. The Declaration of Independence. I heard they even stockpiled morphine during the Cold War."

"We didn't have the raw resources to make it ourselves."

"Whatever." Baldani led him down the hall.

Two more guards stood outside a pair of large, wooden doors. The hinges were polished brass, as long and wide as an outstretched Corgi. Will looked up, carefully studying the individual block letters carved into the arch. Each one was at least three inches deep into the stone, a chisel and hammer digging out the meat of the marble to form the words—

UNITED STATES DEPOSITORY

Baldani asked, "You gonna eye-fuck that sign all day or you wanna go inside?"

The two men muscled apart the wooden doors, and just like that, Will found himself standing at the open vault door. Four armed guards blocked a long, white hallway. The Mint Police. They wore Kevlar vests with the seal of the US Department of Treasury on their chests. Will counted three weapons on each of them, which meant there were probably more he wasn't seeing.

Will had to touch the vault door. The stainless steel was cold under his palm. It was massive, as thick as three grown men and twice his height.

Baldani said, "Takes four people to open that bad bitch. They have to memorize their own combinations, given to them verbally by the Secretary of the Treasury. Nobody can watch them spin it in. Then the wheel gets turned fourteen times to pull back the bolts."

Baldani walked inside, so Will walked inside.

The opulence stopped at the door. Will was reminded of every single government building he'd ever been through. Low ceilings. Exposed air conditioning ducts. White paint that had turned yellow two days after it was slathered onto the concrete blocks. Cracked tile floors. Dirty grout. Multicolored wires leading to no-where.

The temperature dropped another ten degrees. They were going down a steep slope. The walls were lined with smaller versions of the main vault door. Blue signs were posted beside each one. Ribbons hung like police tape from one side of the jamb to the other. Clear plastic envelopes dangled from the ribbons. Will squinted at the lines of type on the papers, but all he saw was row after row of numbers. He assumed they corresponded to serial numbers on the gold bars. He longed to stop and examine each one, to open the stainless-clad doors and peer inside. There were no windows. Each door had two sets of combination dials and a keyed lock straight out of a supermax.

Baldani turned down another hallway. Will looked up. The lights were Xenon, bright enough to pull the intricate details out of the grout between the tiles. He could hear music playing. The sound echoed off the hard surfaces. He took another turn. More vault doors. More signs. More ribbons. Every thirty feet, there was a red phone mounted on the wall, the rotary dial gleaming in the unnatural light.

Up ahead, Baldani turned another corner. The music was louder. Hoobastank, which was some kind of crime. There were no guards this far into the vault. Will guessed there was only one way out and hiding an almost thirty-pound bar of gold on your person would take a special kind of asshole.

"Holy shit." The words slipped out of Will's mouth before he could stop them.

They had reached their first open door. Three men wearing white cotton gloves and face masks were removing bars of gold bullion and stacking them onto a pallet.

"The Reason" stopped mid-whine. Or maybe Will lost his sense of hearing. He had never seen anything like this in his life. This whole time he had been picturing Scrooge McDuck doing his daily money swim when he should've been thinking Minecraft building an entire freaking city.

Baldani said, "Meet the FNG, turdblossoms."

Everyone ignored the douchy introduction. Will stuck his head inside the open vault. The room was around the size of a commercial freezer. No overhead light, but the gold reflected a metallic light that was brighter than any bulb. The bars were stacked on their edges from floor to ceiling in a horseshoe around the periphery. There was enough space for one guy to stand inside and pass the bricks to the guy standing outside. The second guy handed off to the third guy, who gently placed the bars onto a steel pallet.

Will realized he was gawking. He squinted down the hallway as he waited for his pupils to return to a normal size. There was another open door just past the first one. The second team was one man down, but they seemed to be farther along in the process. The guy outside was kneeling down to wipe the bars with a cotton cloth before grabbing two bars in both hands, standing, swiveling around, and handing the bars to the guy inside.

Back-breaking work.

"The read-out for the scale." Baldani tapped the LED display sticking up behind the pallet. "We don't actually count each bar. We weigh the contents of the room, give them a wipe-down, then stack them back inside nice and neat for the next time."

Will nodded, but he wasn't sure that made sense. The vaults were sealed shut, deprived of oxygen. Surely putting the bars outside in the open somehow affected their weight. There had to be moisture in the air, maybe fuzz from the cotton gloves, a stray strand of hair from one of the cleaners. When you were talking millions of ounces, that kind of thing added up.

"Here's where we check the math." Baldani pointed at one of the blue signs. Someone with very neat handwriting had used a white marker to fill in the information. "36,236 bars of gold. Almost twelve billion troy ounces. Gold's going for around thirteen hundred bucks an ounce right now, so that's—well, shit, that's a boatload of fucking benjamins."

A deep voice came from inside the second vault. "$472,238,000."

Will looked past the top of Baldani's stubby head.

The guy inside the vault was hidden from view. Will saw a pair of humongous hands reach out, the seams busted on a pair of cotton gloves. The man's arms were chain-linked with muscle. The faded tan indicated he was more accustomed to working outdoors. He one-handed two bars of gold like they were Lego blocks. Then he took another two bars in the other hand.

"Switch it up, big guy." Baldani snapped his fingers, indicating he meant now. "Lukather doesn't want her new boy breaking a nail."

The man ducked his head as he exited the vault. He pulled down his face mask. White male. Blond hair. Blue eyes. Mid-fifties. Around six-foot-five and two hundred fifty pounds. Built like a linebacker, some might say, but

KARIN SLAUGHTER and LEE CHILD

given the visual reference, Will would describe him as approximately the size of a sealed vault inside of Fort Knox.

The last pieces of the puzzle: Former MP. Currently homeless. Mercenary. Ass kicker. Gold cleaner. Cop Killer.

The stranger from Margrave introduced himself. "Jack Reacher."

2

Reacher was there because of a temporary financial embarrassment. Literally. Nothing sinister. No impending bankruptcy. Purely mundane. Seventeen days earlier he spent more on lunch than he expected, and being a guy who looked ahead when he could, he figured he didn't have enough remaining for all three of a bus ticket, dinner, and a motel for the night. So he went to the ATM.

There was a recent deposit in the sum of $612.14.

Which was unexpected, but easy to explain. It was a message. The six was F, the sixth letter of the alphabet. The twelve dollars was L. The fourteen cents was N. Frances L. Neagley. Not enough to say she was the best NCO he ever had. She was the best soldier he ever met. Maybe the best person. Certainly the closest he ever got to a friend. After the Army she started a hotshot security agency in Chicago. She was doing well. She was connected in all kinds of different places. But now she wanted to talk. That was the message. It was her only way of pinging a guy who lived under the radar, but also ran out of cash now and then. The money was real. She expected him to keep it. Some kind of big-sister thing. Or little sister. Maybe she pitied him.

He called her from a pay phone in a diner.

She said, "I heard a rumor about a guy who knows a guy who wants to talk to you."

He said, "Why me?"

"They need an ex-soldier."

"There are plenty."

"An ex-MP especially."

"There are plenty of retired MPs."

"This is the twenty-first century," Neagley said. "Obviously they wrote a program and scraped the databases and the answer was you. Or someone like you."

"Why would I be in a database?"

"This is the twenty-first century," she said again.

TWO DAYS LATER he was inside the Pentagon. First in a general's office. An impressive guy, but he had nothing specific to say, except to vouch unreservedly for the colonel Reacher was about to meet next. Who had nothing specific to say either, except to vouch unreservedly for the kid in the suit Reacher was about to meet last in line. Seriously. The real deal. Some shadowy agency no one had ever heard of, or ever would. Where the true power was. The people the Pentagon turned to with problems.

The kid turned out to be thirty, and Reacher liked

him a lot. A good age. Reacher remembered it well. The
endless energy. The passion. Plus the guy was smart.
And polite, but in a civilized way, not obsequious. He
was from Georgia, Reacher figured, from his tones and
his cadences. Metro Atlanta, maybe. Like blues music.
The country rhythms, toughened up by the city. A nice
guy, overall.

Plus he had a sense of humor.

He said, "One thing we need to get out of the way."

"What?" Reacher said.

"The mission statement. It makes people laugh."

"Why?"

"I want you to break into Fort Knox."

"I see."

"Actually, I want you to take a job there. Only half
undercover. They want guys like you anyway. You're a
shoo-in."

"The real part or the Disney part?"

"The depository. I'm not real clear exactly what the
job is. It sounds kind of ceremonial to me. Like a ritual.
But that's not the point. As you say, there's more to
Knox than the movies. Overall it's a decent-sized town.
With all the usual problems. Including a network of loan
sharks. Which like all such networks leads back to a
kingpin. Not a very nice guy. A leg-breaker, in fact. But
not the borrower's leg. Questions might be asked at sick
call. Usually the wife's leg, or one of the kids'. Complaints
are never made. For two reasons. One, it's part of the
deal. Two, because of who the kingpin is."

"You know who it is?"

"Yes, we do."

"You say that like it's a bad thing."

"It's a US Army major named David Baldani. He's a big piece of the chain of command down there. No one dares to say a word. Not even when their ten-year-old misses the soccer season."

"So bust him."

"You know how it is," the guy said. "You were in the business. This has got to be tighter than a crab's asshole. We need to see him make a threat. We know he goes to the Burger King from time to time. Perfect place, to meet wives or children. We need to see it happen."

"Why me?"

"Part of the algorithm was based on a note in the file that said it helps to be strong."

"What the hell is this job?"

"Apparently to do with the bars of bullion themselves. Which are heavy. I believe it's some kind of ritual purification. The whole thing is theater anyway. It's a public enchantment. Literally, once. They had to open it up for display—1974, I think. Before I was born."

"I was there," Reacher said. "Some asshole started a rumor there was no gold. He said it was all a lie. People got uneasy. It was a visceral thing. Quiet, but kind of scary. You could see how it could turn ugly. So they started public tours. We were in D.C. very briefly. I was a kid. My dad knew a guy at the head of the line. It was awesome. People felt better after that."

"Knox really hasn't moved on since then," the guy said. "There's splendor and majesty and it's a very potent symbol, but it's still a totally, totally analog world down there."

"Works for me," Reacher said.

"The CO is mad as a box of frogs. She's a full bird named Stephanie Lukather. Baldani is her XO. She insists on calling him Dave in public. Local opinion is split whether that's disrespectful or analog."

"How well does he take it? That's usually a clue."

"Find out for yourself," the guy said. "Baldani is the guy who hires the purification crews. That's his post. You'll be next to him all day long. Follow him to the Burger King. We need to see it happen."

Which was how Reacher found himself cleaning gold, and shaking hands with the new guy, who he needed, because his previous guy had been pulled off the job, unexplained, no reason given, but hey, this was the Army. The job was not rocket surgery, but even so, it helped to have two people. The new guy looked acceptable. Maybe a little surprised. He was a tall guy meeting someone taller. Also a little tense. Maybe worried about something. He said his name was Jack Phineas Wolfe. Presumably ex-Army, a number of years ago, which seemed to be Baldani's fetish, when it came to hiring. His accent sounded a little like the kid in the suit, but older, so from longer ago. More country, less city.

He started with the usual thing about the weight. All the new guys did. About how heavy gold was. About how their gym time was wasted. Then Baldani gave a little lecture about troy weights. From a town called Troyes, in France, way back long ago. The way they measured precious metals. Different ounces, different pounds. Couldn't compare.

Overall, Wolfe learned the job fast enough. But then, so would a chimpanzee. It was not rewarding work. Tolerable as cover for a day or two, but so far Reacher had been there eleven. He was close to maxing out. Close to attracting attention. But Baldani had not yet been to the Burger King. Not one time.

Lunch break was approaching.

Reacher lived in hope.

And for once in his life was rewarded. For the first time Baldani turned away from his usual chow hall and headed for the on-base fast food. Where the families went. Like a decent-sized town. Including the crowds. Following Baldani was easy. On the one hand Reacher had expertise and experience, and on the other Baldani had a kind of smug, sweaty complacency, as if nothing could go wrong in his life.

Reacher wasn't complacent. Same as anyone who had served in West Berlin. The old hands had all kinds of nostrums. One of which was, just because you're following someone doesn't mean someone else isn't following you. Happened all the time.

It happened that lunch break. Reacher glanced back three separate times, and on each occasion he saw the new guy coming after him. He was good, but not the best in all of human history. Of course, it was not actually possible to tell who exactly he was tailing. It was all a straight line. Maybe he was after Baldani also. Maybe he was working a different angle. Tighter than a crab's asshole was a high bar to meet. The more evidence the merrier. Maybe the kid in the suit had sent him too.

Or maybe not. Maybe someone else had sent him. The guy didn't feel like a soldier. Certain words. He was totally willing to take instruction, but not unthinking reflex automatic. Not like the Army. He was a little closed up. He had a personal secret. Not possible, in the big green machine. It would have been beaten out of him long ago.

All in all, Reacher wasn't really sure who he was. Didn't really care, either. The more the merrier. All good. Except Jack Phineas Wolfe was a dumb name to make up. Not plausible. No parent who liked Phineas would put Jack in front of it. Human nature.

Up ahead, Baldani stepped into the Burger King. It was a double-wide store, with three obvious cameras, which meant at least two more not-so-obvious cameras, both of which were quickly identified, and both of which were avoided by keeping right, and then left, and then sitting on a shuttle bench, in line with a large trash can gaudily sponsored by a soda company.

In the corner of his eye Reacher saw the so-called Jack Phineas Wolfe take up station behind the next trash can along. It was sponsored by a different company.

Inside the restaurant Baldani moved between tables. Toward the back. Where it all went wrong. At least for the first split second Reacher assumed it all went wrong. For both of them. Both him and Baldani alike. Because sitting at a table in back was Stephanie Lukather. The batshit crazy CO. The full bird colonel. For once in her life she wanted a burger. That day of all days. A terrible coincidence. Baldani would have to abort. He would have to make his excuses and leave. Nothing would happen. Nothing would be seen. Eleven days, with nothing to report.

But no.

It hadn't gone wrong. It had gone right. Baldani sat down opposite Lukather. They looked at each other in a certain way. A little heart-in-mouth, but mostly practiced. They had done this before. Baldani put his hand in his coat and came out with two envelopes. One held a bulging wad. Unmistakable size and shape. Greenbacks, close to two inches thick. Baldani passed it across the table. Lukather took it.

The second envelope held almost nothing. Just a small hard thing, seeking the corner, heavy enough to slide when the envelope was tilted. About the size of a .45 Magnum round. But flatter. Familiar. Tip of his tongue. Like a dumb quiz show on TV. He would be mad with himself when they said the answer.

Baldani passed it over. Lukather took it.

Out of the corner of his eye Reacher saw the so-called Jack Phineas Wolfe melt away. He himself stayed where he was another long minute. Mostly mad. This was now a whole different circus. This was no longer filling out the blanks in a preprinted boilerplate indictment. This would need a whole new investigation all its own. Could take forever.

He slipped back in the shadows and set out walking, a different route, a little longer, but more interesting, including one spot with a corner and then a blind bumped-in alley entrance, where he stepped in smartly, and waited, until the so-called Jack Phineas Wolfe appeared, looking ahead, a little anxious.

Reacher stepped out behind him.

He said, "Howdy."

Wolfe turned around.

"Oh, hey," he said.

All kinds of things in his face. No real guile or deception. In fact, regret such things were necessary. Deep down, an honest man.

Reacher asked, "What did you see?"

"See?"

"Back there."

Wolfe moved his hands, as if rehearsing a sentence, and then added face and eyes, as if wanting to communicate on every level. For a second Reacher thought the only syllables that could fit the rhythm of the movement were, *I saw you watching Baldani.*

Instead the guy said, "I saw Baldani."

"Doing what?"

"He gave two envelopes to Lukather."

"Contents?"

"Lots of cash in the first."

"Correct," Reacher said.

"A USB drive in the second."

Dumb, Reacher thought. I knew that.

Out loud he said, "I don't know who you are, and I don't want to know. But I assume we're on the same side. So do me one favor. At least tell me your name."

The guy started to say Jack Phineas Wolfe, but Reacher said, "No it isn't."

The guy said, "Will Trent."

3

Back inside the vault, Will carefully wiped dust off the last row of gold bars on the pallet. The overhead light made the Treasury logo and the serial numbers dance across the yellow metal. Inside Will's face mask, his breath had crossed the dew point. The white cotton gloves were glued to his sweaty hands. Lukather had been right about the glamor of the job wearing off quickly. Will's back spasmed as he dead-lifted two bars, turned, then passed them to Reacher.

There was no resting between pivots. Reacher had two hands and one of them was still empty. Not that Will thought of them as hands. They were more like skids on a forklift, because how else could a human being bicep curl almost sixty pounds of gold in each hand like he was lifting sticks of butter?

Will hefted up another two bars, swiveled, and loaded another sixty pounds onto the free skid. He shook out his arms as Reacher all too quickly stacked the bars inside the vault. Megatron wasn't even sweating. Meanwhile, Will's shoulder muscles were clanging like the cymbals on a wind-up monkey.

If he didn't know the guy had perpetrated a murder that took twenty-two years to carry out, Will would've admired his stamina. And also his surveillance skills. Reacher was basically the size of a Ford Pinto, but he'd deftly avoided the security cameras outside the Burger King. There was no way Baldani or Lukather had known that they were being watched.

Did it matter to Will *why* they were being watched?

He hadn't expected to find Reacher singing in a church choir. The man was a murdering thug, so it made sense that he'd be up to murdering-thug things. Maybe the ex-MP was trying to get in on whatever action Baldani and Lukather had going. One of those envelopes had been filled with a shit-ton of money. Will assumed that the Army paid about as well as the GBI, which was to say they all would've been better off flipping Whoppers. Reacher had been out of the service for years. He lived the life of a twenty-first-century hobo. Will could find no record of him owning a house or car. A toothbrush seemed to be Reacher's only possession, and speaking frankly, that thing had to be a germ factory from staying in his sweaty back pocket all day.

Will bent down and lifted another two bars. He swiveled, placing them in Reacher's outstretched hand, then rotated back, silently reminding himself—

Deputy Phillip Michael Deacon had never held his

first grandchild. He had never watched his son play ball.
He had never kissed his wife again . . .

Will passed over another two bars. It had been a risk to give Reacher his real name. Then again, Will had known the guy would not pull out his phone and google him. Hobos didn't have phones. But hobos needed money. Fifteen bucks an hour was more than most Americans could expect for back-breaking labor that would eventually disable or kill them, but Reacher was a criminal, and criminals generally had easier ways to earn cash. So the question was, why was Reacher following Baldani? Was he trying to hone in on whatever action had netted that fat envelope of cash? Or did he want to beat the asshole into the ground the same way that Will did?

Lukather put the goings-on at a whole other level.

But that was a Lukather problem, not a Will problem.

The shady dealings at the base were not part of his mission statement. The only reason he was in this place at this time was to collect evidence that would put Jack Reacher on death row.

Back in 1997, DNA testing had been in its infancy, and onerously expensive for most police forces. Now, you could practically pull a fart out of the crack in a vinyl chair and have it processed within twenty-four hours. Or, for another example, you could extract DNA from three drops of dried sweat that had fallen over twenty-two years ago onto the pages of a book entitled *A Guide to Birds of the Southeastern United States*.

The GBI's paper expert had extracted a complete

profile from the title page of *Chapter 16: Hummingbirds—Beautiful Backyard Warriors*. CODIS hadn't returned a match because Jack Reacher's biometrics were not in the system. The obvious next step was to get a judge to sign a warrant compelling Reacher to give a DNA sample, but not even the most red-blooded, flag-hugging, eagle-shitting judge in the state of Georgia would sign on that dotted line.

The chain of evidence was not at issue. Will had the GBI's Dry Branch evidence log stating that the library book had been in the state's possession since April 16, 1997, the day that Phillip Michael Deacon was shot. He had the publisher's bill of lading and the shipper's records proving that the book had arrived at the Margrave library on that same morning. He had the 1997 forensic report confirming that the only usable fingerprints were found on the book's cover and belonged to the librarian. He had a sworn statement from that same librarian testifying under penalty of perjury that Stranger 1, who was also Stranger 2, was the only patron she had ever seen handle the book.

What Will did not have was a legal foundation to force Jack Reacher to hand over his DNA.

In the arresting-people business, Will had run into what was called the *Combo-Key Paradox*, which went like this: Say there was a bad guy who'd stashed incriminating evidence in a safe. If the safe had a combination lock, the police could not force the guy to give them the combination. But if the safe required a key to open, then the cops could compel the guy to give them the key.

The courts had extrapolated this *contents of the mind* reasoning to everything from opening your phone with your fingerprint to using your biometrics to unlock your computer. As far as self-incrimination went, there was nothing more *self* than your physical person. Your thoughts, like remembering a combination or a phone passcode, belonged solely to you. Your fingerprints, your eyes, your face, the shape of your ears, your walking gait, and especially your DNA—these were yours alone, and the courts were loath to turn them against you without a damn good cause.

Fortunately for Will, there were other ways to legally collect a suspect's DNA.

"Baldani," Reacher said.

Will looked up the hallway for the major, but the douchebag was still outside taking a smoke break with the rest of the cleaning team.

Reacher was apparently taking his own break. The man hadn't spoken a word for over two hours, but now he pulled down his white surgical mask. He leaned against the doorframe, his arms crossed over what had to be a fifty-inch chest.

Will pulled down his own mask. "What about Baldani?"

Reacher said, "I wonder if you guys know more about him than we do."

Will had no idea what he was talking about.

He said, "You first."

Reacher said, "We know the major runs a loan shark network all over town. He breaks little girls' legs. That's why I was sent here. You?"

Will didn't volunteer a justification for his own presence. "Lukather is in on it."

The statement was obvious, because they had both seen the colonel take the envelope, but instead of pointing this out, Reacher peeled off his busted gloves and shoved them into his back pocket.

Will thought about the cotton absorbing the sweat on Reacher's hands. The nasty toothbrush with all of that glorious DNA living inside the bristles. If Reacher discarded any of these items—threw them in the trash, left them on a park bench, abandoned them at the gates of the fort, then legally Will could pick them up and test them for DNA.

Reacher said, "Two envelopes. One full of cash."

Will played along. "Baldani wanted Lukather to take the envelopes from him out in the open. Public place, plenty of security cameras and eyewitnesses."

"Insurance policy," Reacher said. "Mutually assured destruction."

Will felt a cramp in his neck. He wasn't used to having to look up to have a conversation. And the way Reacher pulled out his cotton gloves and started to force them back onto his thick fingers said he had also figured out that Will was not much use to him.

Which was bad.

Will quickly ran through his options. The toothbrush was still in Reacher's back pocket, an area where lingering would be discouraged. Reacher hadn't replaced his gloves for new ones, and judging by the grime, cleanliness wasn't a priority. The surgical mask wasn't going anywhere. Reacher wasn't drinking from a bottle of water. He didn't smoke or chew gum or spit. There were no cuts on his skin, but he probably bled hydraulic fluid anyway. If Will was going to collect a discarded DNA sample without Reacher's knowledge or consent, he would have to keep close and wait for him to make a mistake.

Will said, "We should probably get a look at that USB drive."

Reacher didn't call out the *we*, but he stopped with the gloves, waiting for the rest.

"I don't want to go all Operation Grand Slam here, but Lukather is in charge of all the gold inside this building." He waited, but Reacher didn't take the bait. "Baldani's a blunt object. Lukather is the one swinging him around. Let's say this is bigger than loan-sharking and leg-breaking. That USB drive could—"

Reacher leaned down and gripped one of the bars in his fist. The metal flashed brilliant, casting his face in yellow. He stood up. He showed Will the bar like there weren't eleventy billion more where that came from. He said, "I saw a James Bond movie with a car made of gold. The weight makes me wonder how it got out of the parking lot."

He was talking about Auric Goldfinger's Rolls-Royce. Teenage Will had studied the car more closely than any *Playboy*, and for far longer stretches of time. "It was a Phantom III '37. The last V12 until the Silver Seraph. Coil-spring chassis, semi-elliptical spring in the rear. The brakes would have to be beefed up, but he had the resources."

"I was told ten miles per gallon at top speed. Let's say you get eight touring the countryside. Not counting the extra torque required to haul the gold."

"And the umbrella." Will saw his point. "The tank holds, what—25 gallons?"

"I was told 39.5."

Will worked out a few statistics of his own. "Damn."

Reacher said, "One of us is going to have to hit Baldani."

Will felt his eyebrows touch his hairline.

"Then, the other steps in to break it up."

Will couldn't wait to hear the rest of the plan.

Reacher explained, "Baldani's going to run to the colonel. The colonel will want to talk to the perpetrator and the witness. She'll separate us. One in her office, the other in a different room, to make sure our stories square."

"And?"

Reacher stacked the gold inside the vault. "The USB drive will be somewhere in her office. She can only talk to one of us at a time. Whoever lands in her office needs to look for it. Preferably steal it, but I'm okay with just looking at what's on the drive to make sure she's not planning to make the nation's gold supply radioactive for the next fifty-seven years."

"Fifty-eight, to be exact." Will saw a gaping hole in the plan. "She'll kick us both off the base. If we don't end up in the brig."

"A brig is on a ship. We'd be confined to the stockade, Captain Wolfe." Reacher didn't dwell on Will's mistake. "Lukather told me she's out of here next month, taking full retirement. She's one, maybe two days away from breaking her last record for cleaning the gold. We're her best workers. She wants to go out on a high note. Trust me, she'll give us a stern warning, then put us back to work. This is the Army. What's best for the officer is what happens."

Will thought about it. "What's our squared story?"

Reacher shrugged. "Baldani's an asshole."

He wasn't wrong.

Reacher said, "I'll give him a tap. Just enough to make him bleed."

Will knew there had to be an easier way to get into the colonel's office, but there was a part of Reacher's plan that really appealed to him. "I'll hit Baldani."

"It should be me."

"No, really, I'll do it." Will felt a ripple of anticipation along the back of his punching-hand. "We need to stun him, not turn his jaw into a Hula-Hoop around his neck."

Reacher didn't argue the point, which reminded Will

of the great capacity for violence that raged inside of Jack Reacher. He was an ex-cop who had shot another cop twice in the head. Once a man crossed that line, it was easier to cross the next one, then the next. Jack Reacher had probably spent the last twenty-two years stomping over every line that got in his way.

"Hey, shitbrains." Baldani announced his return by clomping his boots down the hallway like a tiny horse. "Shut your cock holsters and get back to work."

Will waited for him to get close, then punched him in the face.

LUKATHER PACED BEHIND her desk, her mouth set in an angry, straight line. "You want to tell me what the hell happened between you and Baldani?"

Will looked down at his hands. He wasn't trying to show contrition. He was trying to hide his shock. One punch had knocked Baldani out cold, but Will's knuckles looked pristine. There wasn't even a red mark. Did the guy have teeth?

"Soldier?"

Will forced himself to look up.

"You longing for some solitary company?"

Will took her words for a threat. Brig or stockade, his entire mission would be blown if he ended up behind bars. "I apologize for my actions, ma'am. It won't happen again."

"You're damn straight it won't." She undid the top button to her jacket. He could see a river of sweat rolling down her neck. "When I said you were trouble, I didn't mean this kind."

She had more to say, a lot more, but Will tuned her out, thinking about the USB drive. Judging by the shape of the lump in the envelope, it was about the size of his thumb, which was probably why they called it a thumb drive. There were two USB slots on the back of Lukather's computer. Will assumed the system was locked with a password, so looking at the contents of the drive wasn't going to happen. Not that he'd given much weight to that possibility. The most unbelievable scene in any action movie was the part where Tom Cruise jammed the thumb drive into the slot and it slid in on the first try.

"Wolfe." Lukather drummed her fingers on her desk, drawing back his attention. "Can you explain to me in simple English why you hit Baldani?"

Will stuck to the plan. "He's an asshole."

"He was an asshole when you were in here the first time and you didn't pop him." She leaned over her desk, clearly frustrated. "Dave said he was walking down the hall, minding his own business, and you came at him out of nowhere."

Will recalled the last argument he'd had with his girlfriend. "I've heard it said that for a smart man, I can do some pretty stupid things."

"For the love of—" She looked up at the ceiling as if the brown water stain could offer an explanation. Obviously, she didn't get an answer. Or at least not the answer she was looking for. "Stay here."

Will heard the door slam behind him. Heavy footsteps in the hall. Another door was opened, then slammed. She was checking his story with Reacher, just as Reacher had predicted.

Was he right about the USB drive, too?

Will stood from the chair, then went onto the tips of his toes, using his head to pop up one of the panels in the drop ceiling. The flashlight on his phone showed rat droppings, the p-trap for the shower above, and some PEX supply lines that were leaking because some idiot had used push fittings to connect it to galvanized pipe.

That explained why the wood panels on the walls were buckling.

He tilted down his head and let the panel drop into place. He considered his other options. The filing cabinets were locked. There were no pictures on the walls. All he found behind the clock was clock innards. Lukather's desk was the only other place to search. He started with the drawers, where boxes of extra pens and staples were aligned with military precision. He opened each one but found only pens and staples. The ball of rubber bands was filled with rubber bands. The box of tampons was a box of tampons. The family-sized bag of Skittles was filled with Skittles.

He moved on to the piles of folders on her desk, carefully thumbing through the pages, trying to keep the edges squared up as he looked for the envelope with its tell-tale USB lump. He felt underneath the seat of her chair. Then he checked the two other chairs. He rifled the pen cup and paperclip box and found pens and paperclips.

Not even lint.

Will ate some Skittles as he listened at the door. Reacher was taking a hell of a lot longer than Will to relay his version of events. Or maybe Lukather was going back at Baldani. Or maybe she was waiting for the MPs to show up and drag Will to the stockade, because Reacher was a bad guy, but he was also a smart guy, and he had basically talked Will into punching a major in the United States Army.

Will returned to the desk. He tried to put himself in Lukather's shoes. When that didn't work, he opened the drawers again, but this time, he ran his hand along the bottoms.

Bingo.

Will's fingers caught on the edge of an envelope taped to the underside of the file drawer. He got on his knees. He used the flashlight on his phone to look under the drawer. The white envelope was held in place with duct tape. He could tell from the shape that he'd found the wrong one. Lukather had stashed the cash under her desk. At least ten grand, all crisp hundreds, not the crumpled tens and twenties of desperate people, which meant that the loan-sharking money had been cleaned.

Where was the thumb drive?

"—dropped me in a pile of shit." Lukather was out

in the hall. The doorknob turned, but the door did not open. "Does that seem like a me problem or a you problem, Corporal?"

There was a stuttered response before someone took off running down the hall.

Will was sitting down as she entered the room.

Lukather gave him the once-over, certain that something was amiss but unable to say what. Her head went back into the hall. "Reacher, in here."

Reacher looked pained at the thought of entering the cramped room. He was forced to tuck his chin into his chest. He waited for Lukather to sit, then crammed his monstrous form into the plastic chair beside Will. He still had to hunker down under the low ceiling. Hand him a newspaper and he'd look like the Incredible Hulk taking a shit.

Lukather rocked back in her chair. She had unbuttoned her jacket the rest of the way and was full-on sweating now. "Dave, get your ass in here."

The door was already open, but Baldani slammed it back against the wall. Will did a double-take. The guy looked like a cannibal had thrown up on his face.

Lukather said, "All right, boys. Time to make nice."

Baldani balked. "What the fuck?"

"I'm the fuck, Major." Lukather told Will, "I'm not going to waste my breath telling you to apologize, but I expect you to keep your hands to yourself going forward. Understood?"

Will nodded, because he knew if he opened his mouth,

he'd break out into a grin. Here was one of the many pitfalls of going undercover with the bad guys: Will was enjoying this too much. Lukather wasn't the only woman who was going to be jerking a knot in his ass if this went sideways. Will had a real boss back in Georgia who had stuck out her neck to get Jack Wolfe inside of Fort Knox.

He silently reprimanded himself: *Stop the bullshit. Get the DNA sample. Match it to Reacher. Arrest the cop killer.*

Will cleared his throat. "Understood."

"Fuck you, Fobbit." Baldani wasn't going to let this go. "Colonel, you know this ain't right."

"I know that I must do what's right for the depository." Lukather tried to make him see reason. "Dave, there's a chance we can finish tomorrow if we keep these boys moving. Without them, we'll be cleaning another two days, possibly more. I need this job wrapped up pronto. You and I have *both* got better things to do."

"Shit." Baldani's lip was so swollen that he had started to lisp. "Screw breaking the record. We've got another two weeks to finish up, and we don't need trouble right now. *Especially* not now."

She shot him a look of warning. "Careful."

"*Colonel.*" Baldani's eyes ponged between Reacher and Will. He was doing a really bad job of not talking about what he shouldn't be talking about. "We *don't* need *trouble*. Are you *sure* about *this*?"

"As sure as Kilimanjaro rises like Olympus above the

Serengeti." She rocked back in the chair again. Her jacket had bunched up. Will saw the corner of a white envelope peeking out of the inside breast pocket.

The USB drive.

"Playtime is over, gentlemen." Lukather's clipped tone said there was no room for discussion. "Dave, make sure my POV is filled with gas. Reacher, Wolfe, you'll be in the vaults until your shift ends. From the vault, you will go directly to your hotel rooms, where you'll be confined to quarters until twenty minutes prior to the start of your shift tomorrow morning, at which point you will both report to the hotel lobby where you will be escorted back to the vault to continue your work. Once that work is completed, God willing by tomorrow night, neither one of your asses will ever step foot on my base again. Is that clear?"

No one answered.

She straightened her jacket. The envelope disappeared. "I need a 'Yes, ma'am' from every dick-swinger in this room."

Their combined response was a harmony of resignation and contempt. "Yes, ma'am."

4

Trent and Reacher went back to the vault. They got back to work. *Clink, clink.* A fast rhythm. *Her best workers.*

Will said, "The USB drive was still in the envelope. The envelope was in her inside jacket pocket. I saw the corner. I couldn't get near it without being accused of assault."

"What was on it?" Reacher said.

"I don't know. I just told you, I couldn't get near it."

"Speculate," Reacher said. "Purely as a mental exercise. Pretend you're a police officer. Make yourself think like a detective."

"Data."

"About what?"

"I don't know."

"To do with the loans, or separate?"

"Separate," Will said. "If it was an electronic copy of the accounts, it would have been in the same envelope as the percentage cut."

"Excellent," Reacher said. "You're pretty good at this. You should think about taking it up for a living."

"Thank you."

"So what kind of separate thing could it be?"

"Something secret, I guess."

"For what purpose?"

"To sell, I suppose. She's clearly corrupt. She told you she's planning to retire. Maybe she wants a nest egg."

"What kind of secret?"

Will said, "Well, at Fort Knox, I guess there's an obvious answer."

"Except Baldani supplies the thumb drive. How could he? Lukather must know more about the security here. She's the CO. This is the Army. I guarantee Lukather knows a level Baldani doesn't. So the USB isn't Fort Knox security. It's some other secret, that Baldani supplies from below. Which might narrow it down a bit."

They worked on for a minute. *Clink, clink.*

Reacher said, "Where will she sell it?"

Will said, "What's a POV?"

"A privately-owned vehicle."

"Then somewhere far away. She told Baldani to gas it up."

"When will she sell it?"

"I think as soon as she can. She kept it in her inside jacket pocket. Which feels very guarded, in an intimate way, but also temporary. Like it's precious, but it won't be in there for long."

They worked another minute. *Clink, clink.*

Reacher said, "We'll finish this job tomorrow."

"That's why she let us stay. You were right."

"We'll be off the base. If we want to know what she's doing, we have to find out tonight."

"Do we want?"

"This thing could last forever. I hate long engagements. Better to nail her tonight."

"Better for you."

"When do you guys want to do it? Tonight's the night, surely. We can catch her red-handed. Continue the mental exercise. Pretend you're a law enforcement officer of some kind, pretending not to be. You would agree we need to act fast."

"If I was a law enforcement officer, I would probably point out we have no legal means of achieving these objectives. We're confined to quarters tonight, and we have no vehicle, not to mention no warrant or even jurisdiction."

"This is Kentucky," Reacher said. "I'm sure there's some kind of overriding doctrine."

"She'll put a guard on the hotel."

"Two, I'm sure. One front, one back. We're going to need both of them."

THEY ATE AN early dinner in the hotel, Reacher somewhat dutifully, in obedience to his motto, which said eat when you can, because you never knew the next chance. By comparison, Trent ate eagerly. Reacher formed the impression he had been hungry at one time in his life. Maybe as a boy.

Then they stepped out back. The sentry was an MP two-striper, in the new battledress uniform, a pistol on his belt, a cap on his head, an amiable expression on his face, almost jocular, as if there was no us and them, just all soldiers together, and the sentry bullshit was just a formality, like a charade.

Reacher hit him under the chin with a right-hand uppercut. Then he took his gun. Then he wrapped the guy up with duct tape from a service closet. Will Trent didn't like it. A cop for sure. Maybe a human rights lawyer.

Then Reacher walked back through the lobby and did the same thing with the front sentry. Two guns now. Then he stole their car. A drab green Charger, fully loaded. He got right in and started it up. Trent stayed about nine feet away. They spoke through the window.

Reacher said, "There's a Supreme Court ruling. They call it imperfect necessity. It can be okay to commit a small crime to stop a big crime."

"Can be?"

"I'm sure it depends. These people are lawyers. They want to keep working."

Trent didn't answer.

"I'm going now," Reacher said. "I can't afford to miss her."

Trent got in.

LUKATHER LEFT THE base thirty minutes later. Just as dusk was falling. But not only her. Baldani was riding shotgun. And right behind was a whole separate car full of four big men. Then came Reacher, with Trent riding shotgun, a hundred yards back, in a drab green car, which was a color chosen mostly for cheapness, but it was cheap because there was a lot of it available, like economy of scale, and there was a lot of it available because over many decades no other color had ever worked better for merging into the background, especially at dusk. Therefore easy surveillance. It was a part of the country with long roads that led nowhere else. Traffic could hang together for hours. The MP car was a peach. Full of gas, great GPS, shotguns in the trunk, huge amounts of nine-millimeter ammunition.

Will said, "My price estimate keeps going up. She's driving a very long distance, with four heavies to protect her. Therefore she's got something very valuable. Which means her contact will be someone way up the ladder."

"Interested now?" Reacher said.

"As a mental exercise."

"If her contact is way up the ladder, he'll have heavies of his own. It's a status thing. If she's bringing four, he's going to have five or more."

"We won't get close."

"I agree there will be an element of challenge."

JUST BEFORE THE trip turned over a hundred miles, Lukather pulled over into a gravel lot, in front of a roadhouse bar. The chase car pulled in after her. Reacher coasted on, to the next building in view, maybe three hundred yards away, which turned out to be a surplus store, that sold pretty much anything you wanted, as long as you wanted it in camouflage colors. It was closed. Reacher parked there and they walked back.

The roadhouse bar was a commercial operation. Open to all. Except not really. One of those places. The only way Lukather could have felt comfortable walking in was to have five guys with her. Even Reacher would have gotten hard stares. Which he would have returned, which they might have returned again, because it was that kind of place, and after that it would be all about numbers. Altogether safer to stay outside and look in through the windows.

They saw Lukather across a table from a man with pale skin. A blank, hard face. Completely empty, from a lifetime of practice. Russian for sure. He had five men behind him. Lukather's four were arrayed behind her. Baldani was sitting to the side, with another Russian, like chiefs of staff.

Lukather gave the pale guy the USB drive.

The pale guy nodded.

Two of his men lifted two suitcases onto the table. A little bigger than they would let you carry on an airplane.

"Okay," Reacher whispered. "We saw the transaction. So now we need to do this fair but efficient. Agreed?"

"Sure," Will whispered back.

"Fair in the sense that we limit ourselves to strictly proportionate responses only, strictly in self-defense. Agreed?"

"Sure," Will whispered again.

"Efficient in the sense we do it first. Before they're ready."

"That's not self-defense."

"Big picture."

"Jesus," Will said.

"Don't worry about the fine print. Just help me out like a pal from work. It might all come to nothing anyway. I'm not looking for a fight here. I'm hoping they offer a speedy surrender. I really am."

They didn't. The plan was Reacher would line up with the end window, and Trent would sneak inside, whereupon the two divergent lines of fire might force the crowd of thirteen down the side wall, toward the far back corner. Where, huddled together, they would raise their hands and quit.

It didn't work out that way. One of the Russians saw Reacher through the glass. The guy fired instantly. He bust the window and missed by a foot. Reacher fired back through the jagged hole and killed the guy. And then another. And another. Whereupon the return fire grew steady and serious. Apparently serious enough to trigger some kind of an exigent emergency threshold in Trent's buttoned-up thinking. Suddenly he started firing from the flank. After that it got easier. But confused.

Baldani hit the deck. Unhurt. Just hiding. Then a stray ricochet shattered a bracket and a fire extinguisher fell on his head. Guys were going down left and right.

Reacher fought his way in through the window, which was all shredded and shattered by then. Just a hole in the wall. Trent fought his way in from the door. The survivors pushed back to the farthest corner. They started to think about raising their hands. Reacher had them covered.

Then suddenly Lukather rushed for the door. Just Trent in her way. Who reacted perfectly. Instantly, without thinking, he swung a fist at her face.

Then he reacted imperfectly. Some kind of late-breaking gentlemanly instinct kicked in and made him stop the punch dead. It tapped Lukather on the nose. Hard enough to notice. Hard enough to be annoying. Not hard enough to do damage.

Lukather roared in fury and swung a huge right hook that caught Trent on the ear and spun him around. She hammered her elbow into his kidney. She was lining up a forearm smash to his throat when the gentlemanly instinct suddenly kicked back out again, and he threw the punch he should have thrown all along. It caught her full in the mouth and lifted her off her feet in a mist of blood and dumped her down flat on her back.

Reacher shrugged and nodded.

Like, nice work, can't deny it.

Trent slid Lukather over next to Baldani. Which gave them two unconscious forms, and then the pale guy, and two of his stooges, all three of those awake but sullen. They had the USB, and they had the suitcases. Which Trent opened. He brushed his fingers length and width, counting, and he multiplied in his head.

"A million dollars in each," he said.

"Put the USB in one," Reacher said. "Then close them again. Put them neatly by the door. All the valuables in one place."

Trent did.

He said, "Are you going to steal them?"

"Harsh word."

"Are you?"

"Can you stop me?"

"I'm not sure."

"I'm sure not," Reacher said.

"Okay," Will said.

"Of course I'm not going to steal them," Reacher said. "They're evidence. The problem is figuring out who to call. Not the local police department. That's for damn sure. Not all the way the hell out here. This would make their heads explode. If there is a local police department. Not the MPs back at Knox, either. I just hit two of them in the face. They're going to start out by taking a distorted view. Plus, this is a very big deal. Russians, and all. Cash in a suitcase. I think we should call the Pentagon direct."

LESS THAN AN hour and forty minutes later it was all cleaned up. Reacher had given a sworn account. Trent had done the same. The prisoners had been taken into formal custody. The physical evidence had been bagged and tagged and taken away. The meat wagons were coming. Reacher and Trent drove home in the drab green car. Almost a hundred miles. Almost silent.

5

When Will arrived at the depository the next morning, he found that the second shift had motored through the night. Apparently, the cogs continued to turn the wheels fine without Lukather and Baldani cranking on them. The two vault doors that had been open yesterday were locked tight. The ribbons had been re-hung. The pages with the serial numbers dangled in their plastic envelopes. Two new doors were wide open. Two layers of gold bars were already on one of the pallets.

Lukather had been right about one thing. They could finish today if they established a good pace.

Will heard a familiar *clink* of gold hitting gold from inside the far vault. Reacher was already at work, which was not wholly unexpected. Something had told Will that despite the events of the previous evening, Reacher was not the type of man who left a job unfinished.

He didn't have a lot of quit in him.

"Morning," Will said.

Reacher gave him a nod as he placed gold onto the pallet. Left to his own devices, he had tripled up the bars, three in each hand, which was a humiliating data point for Will, who needed both hands to barbell curl 175 pounds. And that was on a good day.

Reacher silently stacked the bars, then turned back into the vault for more.

Will winced as he pulled on his cotton gloves. His knuckles were shredded. Black bruises dotted his skin like ink spots. If the prosecutor needed an impression of Colonel Stephanie Lukather's teeth, Will would be able to supply them. His *never hit a woman* policy had gone to hell the second she had smacked him in the ear and driven a surprisingly sharp elbow into his kidney.

He waited for Reacher to kneel by the pallet, then went into the vault and grabbed two bars with both hands. When he turned, he saw Reacher's toothbrush sticking out of his back pocket.

The bristles. The handle. The plastic. As good as a buccal swab from a DNA testing kit.

Reacher stood up. He stepped into the vault. Will stacked his two bars. They went back and forth, stretching and grabbing and kneeling and stacking, synchronized like a timing belt turning the crank and cam.

Will mentally ran through what had happened at the bar last night. He tried to see all of the angles. Why would Reacher involve himself in something like that? He had risked his life, his health, but for what? Not for the money or for the USB drive. Will had been incapable of stopping him from taking both and leaving the bar. But Reacher had not only stuck around, he had voluntarily given a statement.

That wasn't the behavior of a criminal. That was more like a cop. And Reacher *had* been a cop, but he had just as clearly turned his back on the law.

Will had seldom felt so conflicted.

Here was the problem with Jack Reacher: he was a bad guy who sometimes did good things. Given his itinerant lifestyle, Will thought of him as an American James Bond—not the Bond from the movies but the Bond from the books who was one level up from a street fighter. There was no M to temper his feralness. Reacher did not have a legal license to kill. Or maim. Or shoot people in their knees, which was a really mean thing to do, even to a stone-cold gangster.

To Will's thinking, Reacher was the worst kind of criminal. This wasn't because he was the size of a Mack truck, but because he was smart. Street smart, obviously educated, also methodical and strategic in a way that put him at the top of the top one percent of the criminal class. In most cases, the only thing that cops had going for them was that bad guys tended to be really, really stupid.

Jack Reacher was not stupid.

Will turned away.

"Did you call your people?" Reacher asked.

Will turned back.

"About what?" he said.

"The USB drive," Reacher said. "It's in the system now. It's evidence."

"No," Will said.

"I called CID. Through USACIDC." Reacher was still inside the vault. His mask was pulled down. He leaned against the doorjamb, folded his arms over his engine block of a chest. "That's the Criminal Investigation Division, Captain Wolfe."

"And?"

"Social security numbers," Reacher said. "Turns out Major Baldani's wife works in HR Command. Right here on the base. What they used to call Personnel. She downloads the service numbers of dead soldiers. At least two thousand so far."

"Baldani was married to a human woman?"

"She didn't report the deaths, so the new owners of the service numbers would be eligible for all kinds of benefits."

Will wasn't going to try to pretend he knew what a service number was.

Reacher gave him another assist. "It's the military's version of a social security number. Every soldier is assigned one. Your time of service is attached to the number, and benefits are based on time of service. We're talking pension, disability, exchange privileges, small business loans, VA home loans, GI Bill, life insurance, TRICARE—that's healthcare. You get one of those numbers, you're set for life."

Will felt his stomach turn. Lukather hadn't just tried to sell these soldiers' identities. She had tried to sell their service.

"I'm guessing the contents of that USB drive could bring in tens of millions on the black market. There was only two million in the suitcases. Lukather sold herself short."

Will was glad the woman was going to spend some serious time behind bars. There was not enough money to go around for veterans in the first place. For one of their own to exploit the system felt like treason.

Reacher started to push his mask back up, but Will stopped him with a question.

"Why'd you leave the job?"

Reacher waited.

"You were an MP. I know you quit the Army, but the job gets in your lungs. You can't breathe it out. Why haven't you ever put yourself back on the right side of a badge?"

"'One can't be out in the cold all of the time.'"

He was quoting le Carré. "Don't make me love you."

Reacher said, "I don't like being stuck behind a desk."

"There are a lot of ways to be a cop without sitting behind a desk."

Reacher said, "Like going undercover inside Fort Knox?"

No answer.

Reacher said, "You were never a soldier. You're not

here for Baldani or Lukather. You're here for someone else. You're from Georgia, I'm guessing. Maybe some local police department."

"GBI," Will said. "Georgia Bureau of Investigation. A cold case."

"You should tell me what's on your mind."

Will debated his options, which boiled down to two. One: try to snag the toothbrush fast, and get his face broken into exactly one trillion pieces. Two: come clean and hope for the best.

He asked Reacher, "You ever hear of a town called Margrave?"

"South of Atlanta."

Will waited. When Reacher didn't volunteer anything further, he prompted, "April 16, 1997."

Reacher kept on waiting.

"Deputy Phillip Michael Deacon was shot twice in the head outside the Margrave public library. An eyewitness puts a stranger behind the trigger. A stranger whose description matches yours exactly."

Reacher said, "I was not in Margrave on that date."

"I've got DNA on a library book that proves otherwise."

Reacher didn't seem worried. "What library book?"

"*A Guide to Birds of the Southeastern United States.*"

Reacher's mouth twisted into something that could have been a smile.

Will asked, "Do hummingbirds mean anything to you?"

"They can be ferocious. You get a bully at the feeder,

he'll scare off the other birds or try to stab them with his beak." Reacher added, "It's best to take out the bully as soon as possible. Protect the weaker birds before he starves them all."

Will got the point, but said, "Forensics pulled DNA from three drops of dried sweat on the pages of the hummingbird chapter."

"The toothbrush," Reacher said. "I was wondering why you kept staring at my ass."

Will figured it was his turn to wait for more information.

Reacher asked, "Did you talk to the eyewitness?"

"Died in her sleep two years ago. Natural causes."

Reacher nodded, like that was how it should be. "What do you know about Phillip Deacon?"

"Family man. Spent twenty-one years of his life in uniform, then another twenty-two in a hospital gown." Will explained, "He survived the gunshots, but he was in a coma until two months ago. He died of pneumonia."

"I see," Reacher said. "Thereby converting the charge of attempted murder of a peace officer into murder with aggravating circumstances. A State of Georgia case."

"A death penalty case."

Reacher started pulling off his tattered gloves. "You ever hear of Blind Blake?"

"The blues singer?"

Reacher nodded. "My brother told me that Blake died in Margrave. Actually, he died in Wisconsin, but I never got the chance to tell him."

Will slowly edged back against the wall. He had the fleeting thought that maybe Reacher was taking off his gloves so he could beat Will to death with his bare hands.

Reacher said, "The eyewitness to the shooting. Her name was Beatrice Collins. She was violently raped by Deacon. And badly beaten. Twice. And he made it clear he was going to do it to her again. He told her he really enjoyed it. He told her it got his motor running in a real special way."

Will felt gut-punched.

. . . a wife and teenage boy at home, a married daughter with his first grandchild on the way . . . a violent rapist who had terrorized a woman, probably not just one woman, because Deacon had a badge and a squad car and a boss who always made the point to look the other way . . .

Reacher said, "The first time he raped her, Beatrice was dumb enough to file a report direct with the sheriff. The second time, she was doubly dumb enough to go back to the sheriff again. He told Deacon to take care of the problem. Best all around just to shut her up."

Will's teeth started to ache from clenching his jaw.

. . . Deacon's grandchild was lucky his grandfather had never held him. His son was lucky he had never seen his father in the stands. His wife was lucky that Deacon had never kissed her again, or forced himself on her or preyed on another woman ever again . . .

Reacher said, "I found all this out later. My friend Neagley was starting up a detective agency. It was her first case. She filed a very comprehensive report. As it happened, my brother was in Margrave at that time. He was working. He looked just like me. Actually an inch taller and a tick lighter, but you'd have to see us side by side. He was ex-Army too. He looked like a squared-away guy. Like the Lone Ranger come to town. Beatrice Collins went to him for help. She didn't want to cause trouble. She just wanted it to stop. They were going to meet at the library. Public place. Neutral territory. She was scared. Scratch that. She was terrified. She was a small-town girl with no money and nowhere to turn. The police weren't going to help her. The sheriff once told her he would rape her himself if she told another living soul."

Will knew the crooked bastard of a sheriff was exactly the kind of man who would keep a sexual predator on his payroll. "I'm assuming the sheriff made Beatrice lie in her statement about the shooting. But we're two decades past that. Her partner didn't mention any of this. They were together for fifteen years."

"Victims don't talk about that stuff sometimes, even to their partners. They want to put it behind them. They don't want people to feel sorry for them, or worse, to be blamed." Reacher painted the picture, "Hero cop accused of rape by a grocery store cashier who has a juvenile record for stealing her uncle's car. Whose side do you think the town would've been on?"

Will couldn't argue. People were assholes. "April 16, 1997."

Reacher shoved the cotton gloves into his back pocket.

"Beatrice was late getting to the library. She was nervous. Understandably. My brother was waiting outside when she arrived. Deacon pulled up on the librarian's 9–1–1 call. He grabbed Beatrice and tried to force her into the back of his squad car. My brother didn't like that."

"He shot Deacon in the head."

"Beatrice told Neagley the gun went off by accident."

"Twice," Will said. "That's some accident."

Reacher did not address the inconsistency.

This was where Will and Reacher parted philosophical ways. He said, "Most of the people who get murdered aren't good people. There's a reason they're in a bad situation."

"That's for damn sure."

Will said, "Murder is still murder. 'He deserved to die' is not a valid defense in the state of Georgia."

"I hear it still holds up in Texas."

"What if your brother was wrong about Deacon? What if Beatrice lied?"

"He wasn't and she didn't."

Will wasn't going to lecture a vigilante on the arrogant immorality of vigilantism. "Your brother killed a man in cold blood."

"There's no such thing as cold blood," Reacher said. "Blood is always warm, to a degree. A police officer was stopped from raping a woman for the third time. Maybe worse than that. And exponentially onward, into the future."

Will said nothing.

"My brother is dead anyway," Reacher said. "He was murdered a month later. Also in Margrave, as a matter of fact. No doubt connected to his business there a month before. So you're not going to get your man, however hard you try."

"I didn't find any record—"

"The Margrave sheriff's department didn't keep records of their own crimes," Reacher said. "At that point my brother was working for Treasury. He was a heavyweight figure by then. They took the body away and cleaned up the mess. A week later it was like nothing had ever happened."

Will studied Reacher's face for any signs of deception, but it didn't matter. They both knew he would check out the story.

Reacher said, "Familial DNA."

The guy didn't have a cellphone, but he knew that the similarities in the Y chromosomes of two different males could be used to establish a blood relationship.

Reacher said, "I'm the only one left in my family. I know that my brother was a good man. I don't want to see his name dragged through the mud. But you've made it pretty clear you're not going to drop this case. And I'm not going to get in the way of an honest copper doing his work. Not my thing. So, here."

Reacher had the toothbrush in his hand.

The bristles were crushed from being in his back pocket. Will stared at the tiny sliver of handle sticking out of Reacher's massive paw.

The right thing to do was to collect the evidence, see the investigation through to its logical end, then close the case. Will knew his boss would say the same thing. Just like he knew that she would *also* say it was a waste of resources working a case where the suspect was dead and the victim was equally dead, and also a brutal rapist.

There was a reason why Bond needed an M.

Will crossed his arms over his chest, leaving the toothbrush hanging. "Don't you think it's unsanitary to keep a toothbrush in your pocket all day?"

Reacher returned the toothbrush to its place.

"This one's a mistake," he said. "Usually they come with a cover. Or hotels have them free at the front desk. Like, every day, you can have a new one straight out of the wrapper. Don't worry about my personal standards."

"Sure." Will was suddenly mindful he was lecturing a guy about hygiene when, just this morning, he had eaten the sweat-melted wad of Lukather's Skittles in his pocket.

Reacher began the Sisyphean task of putting on his cotton gloves.

Will leaned down and grabbed two bars of gold. "What do you think is going to happen to Lukather?"

Reacher grabbed six bars, three and three, and waited for Will to stack his. "That's a great question. I heard she's already flipped on Baldani. I heard they're going to give her a deal to testify about the whole scheme."

"Why? They don't need her to make the case. They've got them both dead to rights. They've got the USB and the cash and the bad guy from the bar." Will tried not to groan as he lifted two bars of gold. He thought about Baldani's habit of flicking cigarettes on the ground. The butts were teeming with his DNA. He could take that back to Georgia. And if CODIS returned a hit on Baldani, all the better.

Suddenly he stopped lifting.

He asked Reacher, "How long have you been working here?"

"Twelve days." Reacher disappeared into the vault. "Why?"

"And you work fast."

"I try to give value."

"Therefore you've seen a lot of gold." Will got going again, and stacked his bars on top of the others. They were all stamped with the same seal of the United States Treasury, their individual numbers likely matching the numbers in the plastic envelopes hanging from the ribbons on the doors.

Numbers that hadn't been checked against the gold bars inside.

Gold bars that had been weighed with stray cotton fuzz and strands of hair that would throw the number on the scale over by a few ounces every time.

"It's weird," Will said. "But the thing is, I could swear I've seen these serial numbers before. As in yesterday in the other vault."

"You've seen a lot of numbers," Reacher said. He stacked his bars on top of Will's. "Sixteen digits each.

You and I have stacked and re-stacked 38,492 bars of gold so far. That's 615,872 separate integers. Literally trillions of potential combinations."

Will had to take him at his word. He was pretty good at math, but he wasn't a quantum computer. Though, he did have an incredibly good memory for numbers, and his memory was telling him that the numbers on the bars looked damn familiar.

"I could swear," he said again.

"You good with numbers?"

"In a weird way."

"What was on the second-last bar you just stacked?"

Will recited sixteen digits from memory. Fast and confident. And exactly correct.

Reacher was clearly silently checking him, also from memory. Apparently, he was good with numbers too, in a weird way. He said, "Can I ask you a personal question?"

"What?" Will said.

"Are you a good reader?"

Will didn't answer.

Reacher said, "It often doesn't go together. I knew a few guys. I knew one guy who could tell you the square root of the distance to the sun, but he couldn't read a lick."

"Can you?" Will asked.

Reacher nodded. "I was fortunate. I can read pretty good."

Will didn't answer.

"I agree about the numbers," Reacher said. "They got me thinking. First of all, about how you got here."

"My boss pulled strings."

"How did he know where I was?"

"She."

"How?"

"I put your name in the system," Will said. "A cold case report."

"The GBI system, right? Proudly local. Right now we're in Kentucky."

"Someone made a match."

Reacher nodded.

"Now I'm wondering who," he said. "I'm thinking maybe a kid in a suit. From where the true power is. Which might not be the three-letter agencies anymore. These days it might be the congressional staffs. With seats on all kinds of intelligence subcommittees. Maybe there's a congressman from Georgia. The local half of his brain wants to see the GBI do well, so he lends a helping hand, with information out of the federal half of his brain."

"Which begs a huge question," Will said.

"Exactly. Why send you here in person? A Kentucky SWAT team could have done the job. I could have been extradited. What's another couple months? Your case is already twenty-two years old. Or the MPs could have got me. Why is your actual presence necessary, doing this dumb job as cover?"

Will didn't answer, but he was beginning to think he knew.

"Exactly," Reacher said again. "Because you're good with numbers. Maybe you try to hide it, but you can't. They know. Same with me. They didn't write their program to look for a strong guy. They looked for a guy good with numbers."

Will was quiet a long moment. Then he said, "Did you know that the vault has only been opened to the public one time?"

"1974," Reacher said. "As a matter of fact, the kid in the suit talked about it. A DC attorney named Peter David Beter circulated the theory that the gold had been removed by the Deep State."

"Right, the Deep State. Those guys really get around."

"Do the math," Reacher said. "There's $350 billion worth of precious metals stored here, but the national debt is over twenty trillion. That's already less than two cents on the dollar." Reacher stacked his bars. "This gold is just a symbol. Apparently good enough of a symbol right now. Based on folk memories of 1974. But if people thought even half of these vaults had been emptied out since then, the entire US economy—the world economy—would go into free fall. There'd be rioting in the streets. The banks would fail."

Will passed Reacher on his way to the pallet. They were back on the timing belt. "What I'd do is set up a domino effect."

Reacher caught his meaning. "Night crew moves the gold two doors down. Then we move it two doors down the next day. Same gold. Double-blind. Neither crew knows the other crew is doing it."

Will stood up from the pallet. His kidney screamed around an elbow-sized bruise. Sweat formed a river down his back. They had at least another six hours to go.

He said, "We were sent here to find out."

"I agree," Reacher said. "An obscure congressman from Georgia went to a lot of trouble to bring us here, so we would . . . know, I guess . . . that the nation's gold reserves are terminally depleted, and that fact is being actively hidden by a game of three-card monte. I guess for some reason the guy wants at least one person out there in the world, with that knowledge."

"Two people."

"Only one of us was supposed to survive. Either you would bust me, or I would kill you and escape. He didn't care which, by the way. He was hedging his bets."

"Plus Lukather," Will said. "She must know. She was in charge. Probably she gamed out the way the dominos have to fall so no one person can put together the truth. That's how she's getting her deal. She's trading her silence for her freedom."

"I guess," Reacher said. "So now there are three of us who know."

"The question is why?" Will said. "I mean, okay, we're out there in the world, with the knowledge. So what? What are we supposed to do with it?"

Neither one of them knew.

Read on for a sneak peek at the
latest electrifying thriller featuring
Will Trent by Karin Slaughter

THE LAST
WIDOW

PART ONE

Sunday, July 7, 2019

PROLOGUE

Michelle Spivey jogged through the back of the store, frantically scanning each aisle for her daughter, panicked thoughts circling her brain: *How did I lose sight of her I am a horrible mother my baby was kidnapped by a pedophile or a human trafficker should I flag store security or call the police or—*

Ashley.

Michelle stopped so abruptly that her shoe snicked against the floor. She took a sharp breath, trying to force her heart back into a normal rhythm. Her daughter was not being sold into slavery. She was at the make-up counter trying on samples.

The relief started to dissipate as the panic burned off.

Her eleven-year-old daughter.

At the make-up counter.

After they had told Ashley that she could not under any circumstances wear make-up until her twelfth birthday, and then it would only be blush and lip gloss, no matter what her friends were doing, end of story.

Michelle pressed her hand to her chest. She slowly walked up the aisle, giving herself time to transition into a reasoned and logical person.

Ashley's back was to Michelle as she examined lipstick shades. She twisted the tubes with an expert flick of her wrist because of course when she was with her friends, Ashley tried on all their make-up and they practiced on each other because that was what girls did.

Some girls, at least. Michelle had never felt that pull toward primping. She could still recall her own mother's screeching tone when Michelle had refused to shave her legs: *You'll never be able to wear pantyhose!*

Michelle's response: *Thank God!*

That was years ago. Her mother was long gone. Michelle was a grown woman with her own child and like every woman, she had vowed not to make her mother's mistakes.

Had she over-corrected?

Were her general tomboyish tendencies punishing her daughter? Was Ashley really old enough to wear make-up, but because Michelle had no interest in eyeliners and bronzers and whatever else it was that Ashley watched for endless hours on YouTube, she was depriving her daughter of a certain type of girl's passage into womanhood?

Michelle had done the research on juvenile milestones. Eleven was an important age, a so-called benchmark year, the point at which children had attained roughly

50 percent of the power. You had to start negotiating rather than simply ordering them around. Which was very well-reasoned in the abstract but in practice was terrifying.

"Oh!" Ashley saw her mother and frantically jammed the lipstick into the display. "I was—"

"It's all right." Michelle stroked back her daughter's long hair. So many bottles of shampoo in the shower, and conditioner, and soaps and moisturizers when Michelle's only beauty routine involved sweat-proof sunscreen.

"Sorry." Ashley wiped at the smear of lip gloss on her mouth.

"It's pretty," Michelle tried.

"Really?" Ashley beamed at her in a way that tugged every string of Michelle's heart. "Did you see this?" She meant the lip gloss display. "They have one that's tinted, so it's supposed to last longer. But this one has cherry flavoring, and Hailey says b—"

Silently, Michelle filled in the words, *boys like it more.*

The assorted Hemsworths on Ashley's bedroom walls had not gone unnoticed.

Michelle asked, "Which do you like most?"

"Well . . ." Ashley shrugged, but there was not much an eleven-year-old did not have an opinion on. "I guess the tinted type lasts longer, right?"

Michelle offered, "That makes sense."

Ashley was still weighing the two items. "The cherry

kind of tastes like chemicals? Like, I always chew—I mean, if I wore it, I would probably chew it off because it would irritate me?"

Michelle nodded, biting back the polemic raging inside her: *You are beautiful, you are smart, you are so funny and talented and you should only do things that make you happy because that's what attracts the worthy boys who think that the happy, secure girls are the interesting ones.*

Instead, she told Ashley, "Pick the one you like and I'll give you an advance on your allowance."

"Mom!" She screamed so loudly that people looked up. The dancing that followed was more Tigger than Shakira. "Are you serious? You guys said—"

You guys. Michelle gave an inward groan. How to explain this sudden turnabout when they had agreed that Ashley would not wear make-up until she was twelve?

It's only lip gloss!

She'll be twelve in five months!

I know we agreed not until her actual birthday but you let her have that iPhone!

That would be the trick. Turn it around and make it about the iPhone, because Michelle had purely by fate been the one who'd died on that particular hill.

Michelle told her daughter, "I'll handle the boss. Just lip gloss, though. Nothing else. Pick the one that makes you happy."

And it did make her happy. So happy that Michelle

felt herself smiling at the woman in the checkout line, who surely understood that the glittery tube of candy pink Sassafras Yo Ass! was not for the thirty-nine-year-old woman in running shorts with her sweaty hair scooped into a baseball cap.

"This—" Ashley was so gleeful she could barely speak. "This is so great, Mom. I love you so much, and I'll be responsible. So responsible."

Michelle's smile must have shown the early stages of rigor mortis as she started to load up their purchases into cloth bags.

The iPhone. She had to make it about the iPhone, because they had agreed about that, too, but then all of Ashley's friends had shown up at summer camp with one and the *No absolutely not* had turned into *I couldn't let her be the only kid without one* while Michelle was away at a conference.

Ashley happily scooped up the bags and headed for the exit. Her iPhone was already out. Her thumb slid across the screen as she alerted her friends to the lip gloss, likely predicting that in a week's time, she'd be sporting blue eyeshadow and doing that curve thing at the edges of her eyes that made girls look like cats.

Michelle felt herself start to catastrophize.

Ashley could get conjunctivitis or sties or blepharitis from sharing eye make-up. Herpes simplex virus or hep C from lip gloss and lip liner, not to mention she could scratch her cornea with a mascara wand. Didn't some lipsticks contain heavy metals and lead? Staph, strep, E. coli. What the hell had Michelle been thinking? She could be poisoning her own daughter. There were hundreds of thousands of proven studies about surface contaminants as opposed to the relative handfuls positing the indirect correlation between brain tumors and cell phones.

Up ahead, Ashley laughed. Her friends were texting back. She swung the bags wildly as she crossed the parking lot. She was eleven, not twelve, and twelve was still terribly young, wasn't it? Because make-up sent a signal. It telegraphed an interest in being interested in, which was a horribly non-feminist thing to say but this was the real world and her daughter was still a baby who knew nothing about rebuffing unwanted attention.

Michelle silently shook her head. Such a slippery slope. From lip gloss to MRSA to Phyllis Schlafly. She had to lock down her wild thoughts so that by the time she got home, she could present a reasoned explanation for buying Ashley make-up when they had made a solemn, parental vow not to.

As they had with the iPhone.

She reached into her purse to find her keys. It was dark outside. The overhead lights weren't enough, or maybe she needed her glasses because she was getting old—was already old enough to have a daughter who wanted to send signals to boys. She could be a grandmother in a few years' time. The thought made her stomach somersault into a vat of anxiety. Why hadn't she bought wine?

She glanced up to make sure Ashley hadn't bumped into a car or fallen off a cliff while she was texting.

Michelle felt her mouth drop open.

A van slid to a stop beside her daughter.

The side door rolled open.

A man jumped out.

Michelle gripped her keys. She bolted into a full-out run, cutting the distance between herself and her daughter.

She started to scream, but it was too late.

Ashley had run off, just like they had taught her to do.

Which was fine, because the man did not want Ashley.

He wanted Michelle.

ONE MONTH LATER

Sunday, August 4, 2019

1

Sara Linton leaned back in her chair, mumbling a soft, "Yes, Mama." She wondered if there would ever come a point in time when she was too old to be taken over her mother's knee.

"Don't give me that placating tone." The miasma of Cathy's anger hung above the kitchen table as she angrily snapped a pile of green beans over a newspaper. "You're not like your sister. You don't flit around. There was Steve in high school, then Mason for reasons I still can't comprehend, then Jeffrey." She glanced up over her glasses. "If you've settled on Will, then settle on him."

Sara waited for her Aunt Bella to fill in a few missing men, but Bella just played with the string of pearls around her neck as she sipped her iced tea.

Cathy continued, "Your father and I have been married for nearly forty years."

Sara tried, "I never said—"

Bella made a sound somewhere between a cough and a cat sneezing.

Sara didn't heed the warning. "Mom, Will's divorce was just finalized. I'm still trying to get a handle on my new job. We're enjoying our lives. You should be happy for us."

Cathy snapped a bean like she was snapping a neck. "It was bad enough that you were seeing him while he was still married."

Sara took a deep breath and held it in her lungs.

She looked at the clock on the stove.

1:37 p.m.

It felt like midnight and she hadn't even had lunch yet.

She slowly exhaled, concentrating on the wonderful odors filling the kitchen. This was why she had given up her Sunday afternoon: Fried chicken cooling on the counter. Cherry cobbler baking in the oven. Butter melting into the pan of cornbread on the stove. Biscuits, field peas, black-eyed peas, sweet potato soufflé, chocolate cake, pecan pie and ice cream thick enough to break a spoon.

Six hours a day in the gym for the next week would not undo the damage she was about to do to her body, yet Sara's only fear was that she'd forget to take home any leftovers.

Cathy snapped another bean, pulling Sara out of her reverie.

Ice tinkled in Bella's glass.

Sara listened for the lawn mower in the backyard. For

reasons she couldn't comprehend, Will had volunteered to serve as a weekend landscaper to her aunt. The thought of him accidentally overhearing any part of this conversation made her skin vibrate like a tuning fork.

"Sara." Cathy took an audible breath before picking up where she'd left off: "You're practically living with him now. His things are in your closet. His shaving stuff, all his toiletries, are in the bathroom."

"Oh, honey." Bella patted Sara's hand. "Never share a bathroom with a man."

Cathy shook her head. "This will kill your father."

Eddie wouldn't die, but he would not be happy in the same way that he was never happy with any of the men who wanted to date his daughters.

Which was the reason Sara was keeping their relationship to herself.

At least part of the reason.

She tried to gain the upper hand, "You know, Mother, you just admitted to snooping around my house. I have a right to privacy."

Bella tsked. "Oh, baby, it's so sweet that you really think that."

Sara tried again, "Will and I know what we're doing. We're not giddy teenagers passing notes in the hall. We like spending time together. That's all that matters."

Cathy grunted, but Sara was not stupid enough to mistake the ensuing silence for acquiescence.

Bella said, "Well, I'm the expert here. I've been married five times, and—"

"Six," Cathy interrupted.

"Sister, you know that was annulled. What I'm saying is, let the child figure out what she wants on her own."

"I'm not telling her what to do. I'm giving her advice. If she's not serious about Will, then she needs to move on and find a man she's serious about. She's too logical for casual relationships."

"'It's better to be without logic than without feeling.'"

"I would hardly consider Charlotte Brontë an expert on my daughter's emotional well-being."

Sara rubbed her temples, trying to stave off a headache. Her stomach grumbled but lunch wouldn't be served until two, which didn't matter because if she kept having this conversation, one or maybe all three of them were going to die in this kitchen.

Bella asked, "Sugar, did you see this story?"

Sara looked up.

"Don't you think she killed her wife because she's having an affair? I mean, one of them is having an affair, so the wife killed the affair-haver." She winked at Sara. "This was what the conservatives were worried about. Gay marriage has rendered pronouns immaterial."

Sara was having a hard time tracking until she realized that Bella was pointing to an article in the newspaper. Michelle Spivey had been abducted from a shopping center parking lot four weeks ago. She was a scientist with the Centers for Disease Control, which meant that the FBI had taken over the investigation. The photo in the paper was from Michelle's driver's license.

It showed an attractive woman in her late thirties with a spark in her eye that even the crappy camera at the DMV had managed to capture.

Bella asked, "Have you been following the story?"

Sara shook her head. Unwanted tears welled into her eyes. Her husband had been killed five years ago. The only thing she could think of that would be worse than losing someone she loved was never knowing whether or not that person was truly gone.

Bella said, "I'm going with murder for hire. That's what usually turns out to be the case. The wife traded up for a newer model and had to get rid of the old one."

Sara should've dropped it because Cathy was clearly getting worked up. But, because Cathy was clearly getting worked up, Sara told Bella, "I dunno. Her daughter was there when it happened. She saw her mother being dragged into a van. It's probably naive to say this, but I don't think her other mother would do something like that to their child."

"Fred Tokars had his wife shot in front of his kids."

"That was for the life insurance, I think? Plus, wasn't his business shady, and there was some mob connection?"

"And he was a man. Don't women tend to kill with their hands?"

"For the love of God." Cathy finally broke. "Could we please not talk about murder on the Lord's day? And Sister, you of all people should not be discussing cheating spouses."

Bella rattled the ice in her empty glass. "Wouldn't a mojito be nice in this heat?"

Cathy clapped her hands together, finished with the green beans. She told Bella, "You're not helping."

"Oh, Sister, one should never look to Bella for help."

Sara waited for Cathy to turn her back before she wiped her eyes. Bella hadn't missed her sudden tears, which meant that as soon as Sara had left the kitchen, they would both be talking about the fact that she had been on the verge of crying because—why? Sara was at a loss to explain her weepiness. Lately, anything from a sad commercial to a love song on the radio could set her off.

She picked up the newspaper and pretended to read the story. There were no updates on Michelle's disappearance. A month was too long. Even her wife had stopped pleading for her safe return and was begging whoever had taken Michelle to please just let them know where they could find the body.

Sara sniffed. Her nose had started running. Instead of reaching for a paper napkin from the pile, she used the back of her hand.

She didn't know Michelle Spivey, but last year she had briefly met her wife, Theresa Lee, at an Emory Medical School alumni mixer. Lee was an orthopedist and professor at Emory. Michelle was an epidemiologist at the CDC. According to the article, the two were married in 2015, which likely meant they'd tied the knot as soon as they were legally able. They had been together for fifteen years before that. Sara assumed that after two decades, they'd figured out the two most common causes of divorce: the acceptable temperature setting for the thermostat and what level of criminal act it was to pretend you didn't know the dishwasher was ready to be emptied.

Then again, she was not the marriage expert in the room.

"Sara?" Cathy had her back to the counter, arms crossed. "I'm just going to be blunt."

Bella chuckled. "Give it a try."

"It's okay to move on," Cathy said. "Make a new life for yourself with Will. If you're truly happy, then be truly happy. Otherwise, what the hell are you waiting for?"

Sara carefully folded the newspaper. Her eyes returned to the clock.

1:43 p.m.

Bella said, "I did like Jeffrey, rest his soul. He had that swagger. But Will is so sweet. And he does love you, honey." She patted Sara's hand. "He really does."

Sara chewed her lip. Her Sunday afternoon was not going to turn into an impromptu therapy session. She didn't need to work out her feelings. She was caught in the reverse problem of every romantic comedy's first act: she had already fallen in love with Will, but she wasn't sure how to love him.

Will's social awkwardness she could deal with, but his inability to communicate had nearly been the end of them. Not just once or twice, but several times. Initially,

Sara had persuaded herself he was trying to show his best side. That was normal. She had let six months pass before she'd worn her real pajamas to bed.

Then a year had gone by and he was still keeping things to himself. Stupid things that didn't matter, like not calling to tell her that he was going to have to work late, that his basketball game was running long, that his bike had broken down halfway into his ride, that he'd volunteered his weekend to help a friend move. He always looked shocked when she was mad at him for not communicating these things. She wasn't trying to keep track of him. She was trying to figure out what to order for dinner.

As annoying as those interactions were, there were other things that really mattered. Will didn't lie so much as find clever ways to not tell her the truth—whether it had to do with a dangerous work situation or some awful detail about his childhood or, worse, a recent atrocity committed by his nasty, narcissistic bitch of an ex-wife.

Logically, Sara understood the genesis of Will's behavior. He had spent his childhood in the foster care system, where, if he wasn't being neglected, he was being abused. His ex-wife had weaponized his emotions against him. He had never really been in a healthy relationship. There were some truly heinous skeletons lurking in his past. Maybe Will felt like he was protecting Sara. Maybe he felt like he was protecting himself. The point was that she had no fucking idea which one it was because he wouldn't acknowledge the problem existed.

"Sara, honey," Bella said. "I meant to tell you—the other day, I was thinking about when you lived here back when you were in school. Do you remember that, sugar?"

Sara smiled at the memory of her college years, but then the edges of her lips started to give when she caught the look that was exchanged between her aunt and mother.

A hammer was about to drop.

They had lured her here with the promise of fried chicken.

Bella said, "Baby, I'm gonna be honest. This old place is too much house for your sweet Aunt Bella to handle. What do you think of moving back in?"

Sara laughed, but then she saw that her aunt was serious.

Bella said, "Y'all could fix up the place, make it your own."

Sara felt her mouth moving, but she had no words.

"Honey." Bella held on to Sara's hand. "I always meant to leave it to you in my will, but my accountant says the tax situation would be better if I transferred it to you now through a trust. I've already put down a deposit on a condo downtown. You and Will can move in by Christmas. That foyer takes a twenty-foot tree, and there's plenty of room for—"

Sara experienced a momentary loss of hearing.

She had always loved the grand old Georgian, which was built just before the Great Depression. Six bedrooms, five bathrooms, a two-bedroom carriage house, a tricked-out garden shed, three acres of grounds in one of the state's most affluent zip codes. A ten-minute drive would take you downtown. A ten-minute stroll would have you at the center of the Emory University campus. The neighborhood was one of the last commissions Frederick Law Olmstead took before his death, and parks and trees blended beautifully into the Fernbank Forest.

It was an enticing offer until the numbers started scrolling through her head.

Bella hadn't replaced anything since the 1980s. Central heating and air. Plumbing. Electrical. Plaster repairs. New windows. New roof. New gutters. Wrangling with the Historical Society over minute architectural details. Not to mention the time they would lose because Will would want to do all the work himself and Sara's scant free evenings and long, lazy weekends would turn into arguments about paint colors and money.

Money.

That was the real obstacle. Sara had a lot more money than Will. The same had been true of her marriage. She would never forget the look on Jeffrey's face the first time he'd seen the balance in her trading account. Sara had actually heard the squeaking groan of his testicles retracting into his body. It had taken a hell of a lot of suction to get them back out again.

Bella was saying, "And of course I can help with any taxes, but—"

"Thank you." Sara tried to dive in. "That's very generous, but—"

"It could be a wedding present." Cathy smiled sweetly as she sat down at the table. "Wouldn't that be lovely?"

Sara shook her head, but not at her mother. What was wrong with her? Why was she worrying about Will's reaction? She had no idea how much money he had. He paid cash for everything. Whether this was because he didn't believe in credit cards or because his credit was screwed up was another conversation that they were not having.

"What was that?" Bella had her head tilted to the side. "Did y'all hear something? Like firecrackers? Or something?"

Cathy ignored her. "You and Will can make this your home. And your sister can take the apartment over the garage."

Sara saw the hammer make its final blow. Her mother wasn't merely trying to control Sara's life. She wanted to throw in Tessa for good measure.

Sara said, "I don't think Tess wants to live over another garage."

Bella asked, "Isn't she living in a mud hut now?"

"Sissy, hush." Cathy asked Sara, "Have you talked to Tessa about moving home?"

"Not really," Sara lied. Her baby sister's marriage was falling apart. She Skyped with her at least twice a day, even though Tessa was living in South Africa. "Mama, you have to let this go. This isn't the 1950s. I can pay my own bills. My retirement is taken care of. I don't need to be legally bound to a man. I can take care of myself."

Cathy's expression lowered the temperature in the room. "If that's what you think marriage is, then I have nothing else to say on the matter." She pushed herself up from the table and returned to the stove. "Tell Will to wash up for dinner."

Sara closed her eyes so that she wouldn't roll them. She stood up and left the kitchen.

Her footsteps echoed through the cavernous living room as she skirted the periphery of the ancient Oriental rug. She stopped at the first set of French doors. She pressed her forehead against the glass. Will was happily pushing the lawn mower into the shed. The yard looked spectacular. He had even trimmed the boxwoods into neat rectangles. The edging showed a surgical precision.

What would he say to a 2.5 million-dollar fixer-upper?

Sara wasn't even sure she wanted such a huge responsibility. She had spent the first few years of her marriage remodeling her tiny craftsman bungalow with Jeffrey. Sara keenly recalled the physical exhaustion from stripping wallpaper and painting stair spindles, and the excruciating agony of knowing that she could just write a check and let someone else do it, but her husband was a stubborn, stubborn man.

Her husband.

That was the third rail her mother had been reaching

for in the kitchen: Did Sara love Will the same way she had loved Jeffrey, and if she did, why wasn't she marrying him, and if she didn't, why was she wasting her time?

All good questions, but Sara found herself caught in a Scarlett O'Hara loop of promising herself that she would think about it tomorrow.

She shouldered open the door and was met by a wall of heat. Thick humidity made the air feel like it was sweating. Still, she reached up and took the band out of her hair. The added layer on the back of her neck was like a heated oven mitt. Except for the smell of fresh grass, she might as well be walking into a steam room. She trudged up the hill. Her sneakers slipped on some loose rocks. Bugs swarmed around her face. She swatted at them as she walked toward what Bella called the shed but was actually a converted barn with a bluestone floor and space for two horses and a carriage.

The door was open. Will stood in the middle of the room. His palms were pressed to the top of the workbench as he stared out the window. There was a stillness to him that made Sara wonder if she should interrupt. Something had been bothering him for the last two months. She could feel it edging into almost every part of their lives. She had asked him about it. She had given him space to think about it. She had tried to fuck it out of him. He kept insisting that he was fine, but then she'd catch him doing what he was doing now: staring out a window with a pained expression on his face.

Sara cleared her throat.

Will turned around. He'd changed shirts, but the heat had already plastered the material to his chest. Pieces of grass were stuck to his muscular legs. He was long and lean and the smile that he gave Sara momentarily made her forget every single problem she had with him.

He asked, "Is it time for lunch?"

She looked at her watch. "It's one forty-six. We have exactly fourteen minutes of calm before the storm."

His smile turned into a grin. "Have you seen the shed? I mean, really seen it?"

Sara thought it was pretty much a shed, but Will was clearly excited.

He pointed to a partitioned area in the corner. "There's a urinal over there. An actual, working urinal. How cool is that?"

"Awesome," she muttered in a non-awesome way.

"Look how sturdy these beams are." Will was six-four, tall enough to grab the beam and do a few pull-ups. "And look over here. This TV is old, but it still works. And there's a full refrigerator and microwave over here where I guess the horses used to live."

She felt her lips curve into a smile. He was such a city boy he didn't know that it was called a stall.

"And the couch is kind of musty, but it's really comfortable." He bounced onto the torn leather couch, pulling her down beside him. "It's great in here, right?"

Sara coughed at the swirling dust. She tried not to

connect the stack of her uncle's old *Playboy*s to the creaking couch.

Will asked, "Can we move in? I'm only halfway kidding."

Sara bit her lip. She didn't want him to be kidding. She wanted him to tell her what he wanted.

"Look, a guitar." He picked up the instrument and adjusted the tension on the strings. A few strums later and he was making recognizable sounds. And then he turned it into a song.

Sara felt the quick thrill of surprise that always came with finding out something new about him.

Will hummed the opening lines of Bruce Springsteen's "I'm on Fire."

He stopped playing. "That's kind of gross, right? 'Hey little girl is your daddy home?'"

"How about 'Girl, You'll Be a Woman Soon'? Or 'Don't Stand So Close to Me'? Or the opening line to 'Sara Smile'?"

"Damn." He plucked at the guitar strings. "Hall and Oates, too?"

"Panic! At the Disco has a better version." Sara watched his long fingers work the strings. She loved his hands. "When did you learn to play?"

"High school. Self-taught." Will gave her a sheepish look. "Think of every stupid thing a sixteen-year-old boy would do to impress a sixteen-year-old girl and I know how to do it."

She laughed, because it wasn't hard to imagine. "Did you have a fade?"

"Duh." He kept strumming the guitar. "I did the Pee-wee Herman voice. I could flip a skateboard. Knew all the words to 'Thriller.' You should've seen me in my acid-washed jeans and Nember's Only jacket."

"Nember?"

"Dollar Store brand. I didn't say I was a millionaire." He looked up from the guitar, clearly enjoying her amusement. But then he nodded toward her head, asking, "What's going on up there?"

Sara felt her earlier weepiness return. Love overwhelmed her. He was so tuned into her feelings. She so desperately wanted him to accept that it was natural for her to be tuned into his.

Will put down the guitar. He reached up to her face, used his thumb to rub the worry out of her brow. "That's better."

Sara kissed him. Really kissed him. This part was always easy. She ran her fingers through his sweaty hair. Will kissed her neck, then lower. Sara arched into him. She closed her eyes and let his mouth and hands smooth away all of her doubts.

They only stopped because the couch gave a sudden, violent shudder.

Sara asked, "What the hell was that?"

Will didn't trot out the obvious joke about his ability to make the earth move. He looked under the couch. He stood up, checking the beams overhead, rapping his knuckles on the petrified wood. "Remember that earthquake in Alabama a few years back? That felt the same, but stronger."

Sara straightened her clothes. "The country club does fireworks displays. Maybe they're testing out a new show?"

"In broad daylight?" Will looked dubious. He found his phone on the workbench. "There aren't any alerts." He scrolled through his messages, then made a call. Then another. Then he tried a third number. Sara waited, expectant, but Will ended up shaking his head. He held up the phone so she could hear the recorded message saying that all circuits were busy.

She noted the time in the corner of the screen.

1:51 p.m.

She told Will, "Emory has an emergency siren. It goes off when there's a natural disast—"

Boom!

The earth gave another violent shake. Sara had to steady herself against the couch before she could follow Will into the backyard.

He was looking up at the sky. A plume of dark smoke curled up behind the tree line. Sara was intimately familiar with the Emory University campus.

Fifteen thousand students.

Six thousand faculty and staff members.

Two ground-shaking explosions.

"Let's go." Will jogged toward the car. He was a special agent with the Georgia Bureau of Investigation. Sara was a doctor. There was no need to have a discussion about what they should do.

"Sara!" Cathy called from the back door. "Did you hear that?"

"It's coming from Emory." Sara ran into the house to find her car keys. She felt her thoughts spinning into dread. The urban campus sprawled over six hundred acres. The Emory University Hospital. Egleston Children's Hospital. The Centers for Disease Control. The National Public Health Institute. The Yerkes National Primate Research Center. The Winship Cancer Institute. Government labs. Pathogens. Viruses. Terrorist attack? School shooter? Lone gunman?

"Could it be the bank?" Cathy asked. "There were those bank robbers who tried to blow up the jail."

Martin Novak. Sara knew there was an important meeting taking place downtown, but the prisoner was stashed in a safe house well outside of the city.

Bella said, "Whatever it is, it's not on the news yet." She had turned on the kitchen television. "I've got Buddy's old shotgun around here somewhere."

Sara found her key fob in her purse. "Stay inside." She grabbed her mother's hand, squeezed it tight. "Call Daddy and Tessa and let them know you're okay."

She put her hair up as she walked toward the door. She froze before she reached it.

They had all frozen in place.

The deep, mournful wail of the emergency siren filled the air.

Read on for a sneak peek at
Lee Child's latest thrilling novel

BLUE MOON

A JACK REACHER NOVEL

Out now from Delacorte Press

1

The city looked small on a map of America. It was just a tiny polite dot, near a red threadlike road that ran across an otherwise empty half inch of paper. But up close and on the ground it had half a million people. It covered more than a hundred square miles. It had nearly a hundred and fifty thousand households. It had more than two thousand acres of parkland. It spent half a billion dollars a year, and raised almost as much through taxes and fees and charges. It was big enough that the police department was twelve hundred strong.

And it was big enough that organized crime was split two separate ways. The west of the city was run by Ukrainians. The east was run by Albanians. The demarcation line between them was gerrymandered as tight as a congressional district. Nominally it followed Center Street, which ran north to south and divided the city in half, but it zigged and zagged and ducked in and out to include or exclude specific blocks and parts of specific

---

neighborhoods, wherever it was felt historic precedents justified special circumstances. Negotiations had been tense. There had been minor turf wars. There had been some unpleasantness. But eventually an agreement had been reached. The arrangement seemed to work. Each side kept out of the other's way. For a long time there had been no significant contact between them.

Until one morning in May. The Ukrainian boss parked in a garage on Center Street, and walked east into Albanian territory. Alone. He was fifty years old and built like a bronze statue of an old hero, tall, hard, and solid. He called himself Gregory, which was as close as Americans could get to pronouncing his given name. He was unarmed, and he was wearing tight pants and a tight T-shirt to prove it. Nothing in his pockets. Nothing concealed. He turned left and right, burrowing deep, heading for a backstreet block, where he knew the Albanians ran their businesses out of a suite of offices in back of a lumber yard.

He was followed all the way, from his first step across the line. Calls were made ahead, so that when he arrived he was faced by six silent figures, all standing still in the space between the sidewalk and the lumber yard's gate, like chess pieces in a defensive formation. He stopped and held his arms out from his sides. He turned around slowly, a full 360, his arms still held wide. Tight pants, tight T-shirt. No lumps. No bulges. No knife. No gun. Unarmed, in front of six guys who undoubtedly weren't. But he wasn't worried. To attack him unprovoked was a step the Albanians wouldn't take. He knew that. Courtesies had to be observed. Manners were manners.

One of the six silent figures stepped up. Partly a blocking manuever, partly ready to listen.

Gregory said, "I need to speak with Dino."

Dino was the Albanian boss.

The guy said, "Why?"

"I have information."

"About what?"

"Something he needs to know."

"Don't you have his phone number?"

"This is a thing that needs to be said face to face."

"Does it need to be said right now?"

"Yes, it does."

The guy said nothing for a spell, and then he turned and ducked through a personnel door set low in a metal roll-up gate. The other five guys formed up tighter, to replace his missing presence. Gregory waited. The five guys watched him, part wary, part fascinated. It was a unique occasion. Once in a lifetime. Like seeing a unicorn. The other side's boss. Right there. Previous negotiations had been held on neutral ground, on a golf course way out of town, on the other side of the highway.

Gregory waited. Five long minutes later the guy came back out through the personnel door. He left it open. He gestured. Gregory walked forward and ducked and stepped inside. He smelled fresh pine and heard the whine of a saw.

The guy said, "We need to search you for a wire."

Gregory nodded and stripped off his T shirt. His torso was thick and hard and matted with hair. No wire. The guy checked the seams in his T shirt and handed it back. Gregory put it on and ran his fingers through his hair.

The guy said, "This way."

He led Gregory deep into the corrugated shed. The other five guys followed. They came to a plain metal door. Beyond it was a windowless space set up like a boardroom. Four laminate tables had been pushed together end to end, like a barrier. In a chair in the center on the far side was Dino. He was younger than Gregory by a year or two, and shorter by an inch or two, but wider. He had dark hair, and a knife scar on the left side of his face, shorter above the eyebrow and longer from cheekbone to chin, like an upside-down exclamation point.

The guy who had done the talking pulled out a chair for Gregory opposite Dino, and then tracked around and sat down at Dino's right hand, like a faithful lieutenant. The other five split three and two and sat alongside them. Gregory was left alone on his side of the table, facing seven blank faces. At first no one spoke. Then eventually Dino asked, "To what do I owe this great pleasure?"

Manners were manners.

Gregory said, "The city is about to get a new police commissioner."

"We know this," Dino said.

"Promoted from within."

"We know this," Dino said again.

"He has promised a crackdown, against both of us."

"We know this," Dino said, for the third time.

"We have a spy in his office."

Dino said nothing. He hadn't known that.

Gregory said, "Our spy found a secret file on a stand-alone hard drive hidden in a drawer."

"What file?"

"His operational plan for cracking down on us."

"Which is what?"

"It's short on detail," Gregory said. "In parts it's extremely sketchy. But not to worry. Because day by day and week by week he's filling in more and more parts of the puzzle. Because he's getting a constant stream of inside information."

"From where?"

"In the back of the file was a list."

"A list of what?"

"His confidential informants," Gregory said.

"Snitches?"

"Traitors."

"And?"

"There were four names on the list."

"And?"

"Two of them were my own men," Gregory said.

No one spoke.

Eventually Dino asked, "What have you done with them?"

"I'm sure you can imagine."

Again no one spoke.

Then Dino asked, "Why are you telling me this? What has this got to do with me?"

"The other two names on the list are your men."

Silence.

Gregory said, "We share a predicament."

Dino asked, "Who are they?"

Gregory said the names.

Dino said, "Why are you telling me about them?"

"Because we have an agreement," Gregory said. "I'm a man of my word."

"You stand to benefit enormously if I go down. You would run the whole city."

"I stand to benefit only on paper," Gregory said. "Suddenly I realize I should be happy with the status quo. Where would I find enough honest men to run your operations? Apparently I can't even find enough to run my own."

"And apparently neither can I."

"So we'll fight each other tomorrow. Today we'll respect the agreement. I'm sorry to have brought you embarrassing news. But I embarrassed myself also. In front of you. I hope that counts for something. We share this predicament."

Dino nodded. Said nothing.

Gregory said, "I have a question."

"Then ask it," Dino said.

"Would you have told me, like I told you, if the spy had been yours, and not mine?"

Dino was quiet a very long time.

Then he said, "Yes, and for the same reasons. We have an agreement. And if we both have names on their list, then neither one of us should be in a hurry to get foolish."

Gregory nodded and stood up.

Dino's right-hand man stood up to show him out.

Dino asked, "Are we safe now?"

"We are from my side," Gregory said. "I can guarantee that. As of six o'clock this morning. We have a guy at the city crematorium. He owes us money. He was willing to light the fire a little early today."

Dino nodded and said nothing.

Gregory asked, "Are we safe from your side?"

"We will be," Dino said. "By tonight. We have a guy at the car crushing plant. He owes us money, too."

The right-hand man showed Gregory out, across the deep shed to the low door in the roll-up gate, and out to the bright May morning sunshine.

At that same moment Jack Reacher was seventy miles away, in a Greyhound bus, on the interstate highway. He was on the left side of the vehicle, toward the rear, in the window seat over the axle. There was no one next to him. Altogether there were twenty-nine other passengers. The usual mixture. Nothing special. Except for one particular situation, which was mildly interesting. Across the aisle and one row in front was a guy asleep with his head hanging down. He had gray hair overdue for a trim, and loose gray skin, as if he had lost a lot of weight. He could have been seventy years old. He was wearing a short blue zip jacket. Some kind of heavy cotton. Maybe waterproof. The butt end of a fat envelope was sticking out of the pocket.

It was a type of envelope Reacher recognized. He had seen similar items before. Sometimes, if their ATM was busted, he would step inside a bank branch and get cash with his card from the teller, directly across the counter. The teller would ask how much he wanted, and he would think, well, if ATM reliability was on the decline, then maybe he should get a decent wad, to be on the safe side, and he would ask for two or three times what he normally took. A large sum. Whereupon the teller would ask if he wanted an envelope with that. Sometimes Reacher said yes, just for the sake of it, and he would get his wad in an envelope exactly like the one sticking out of the sleeping guy's pocket. Same thick paper, same size, same proportions, same bulge, same heft. A few hundred dollars, or a few thousand, depending on the mix of bills.

Reacher wasn't the only one who had seen it. The guy dead ahead had seen it, too. That was clear. He was taking a big interest. He was glancing across and down, across and down, over and over. He was a lean guy with greasy hair and a goatee beard. Thirty-something, in a jeans jacket. Glancing, thinking, planning. Licking his lips.

The bus rolled on. Reacher took turns watching out

the window, and watching the envelope, and watching the guy watching the envelope.

GREGORY CAME OUT of the Center Street garage and drove back into safe Ukrainian territory. His offices were in back of a taxi company, across from a pawn shop, next to a bail bond operation, all of which he owned. He parked and went inside. His top guys were waiting there. Four of them, all similar to each other, and to him. Not related in the traditional family sense, but they were from the same towns and villages and prisons back in the old country, which was probably even better.

They all looked at him. Four faces, eight wide eyes, but only one question.

Which he answered.

"Total success," he said. "Dino bought the whole story. That's one dumb donkey, let me tell you. I could have sold him the Brooklyn Bridge. The two guys I named are history. He'll take a day to reshuffle. Opportunity knocks, my friends. We have about twenty-four hours. Their flank is wide open."

"That's Albanians for you," his own right-hand man said.

"Where did you send our two?"

"The Bahamas. There's a casino guy who owes us money. He has a nice hotel."

THE GREEN FEDERAL signs on the highway shoulder showed a city coming up. The first stop of the day.

Reacher watched the guy with the goatee map out his play. There were two unknowns. Was the guy with the money planning to get out there? And if not, would he wake up anyway, with the slowing and the turning and the jolting?

Reacher watched. The bus took the exit. A state four-lane then carried it south, through flat land moist with recent rain. The ride was smooth. The guy with the money stayed asleep. The guy with the goatee kept on watching him. Reacher guessed his plan was made. He wondered how good of a plan it was. The smart play would be pickpocket the envelope pretty soon, conceal it well, and then aim to get out of the bus as soon as it stopped. Even if the guy woke up short of the depot, he would be confused at first. Maybe he wouldn't even notice the envelope was gone. Not right away. And even when he did, why would he jump straight to conclusions? He would figure it had fallen out. He would spend a minute looking on the seat, and under it, and under the seat in front, because he might have kicked it in his sleep. Only after all of that would he start to look around, questioningly. By which time the bus would be stopped and people would be getting up and getting out and getting in. The aisle would be jammed. A guy could slip away, no problem. That was the smart play.

Did the guy know it?

Reacher never found out.

The guy with the money woke up too soon.

The bus slowed, and then stopped for a light with a

hiss of brakes, and the guy's head jerked up, and he blinked, and patted his pocket, and shoved the envelope down deeper, where no one could see it.

Reacher sat back.

The guy with the beard sat back.

The bus rolled on. There were fields either side, dusted pale green with spring. Then came the first commercial lots, for farm equipment, and domestic automobiles, all spread over huge acreages, with hundreds of shiny machines lined up under flags and bunting. Then came office parks, and a giant out-of-town supermarket. Then came the city itself. The four-lane narrowed to two. Up ahead were taller buildings. But the bus turned off left and tracked around, keeping a polite distance behind the high-rent districts, until half a mile later it arrived at the depot. The first stop of the day. Reacher stayed in his seat. His ticket was good for the end of the line.

The guy with the money stood up.

He kind of nodded to himself, and hitched up his pants, and tugged down his jacket. All the things an old guy does, when he's about to get out of a bus.

He stepped into the aisle, and shuffled forward. No bag. Just him. Gray hair, blue jacket, one pocket fat, one pocket empty.

The guy with the goatee got a new plan.

It came on him all of a sudden. Reacher could practically see the gears spinning in the back of his head. Coming up cherries. A sequence of conclusions built on a chain of assumptions. Bus depots were never in the nice part of town. The exit doors would give out onto cheap streets, the backs of other buildings, maybe vacant lots, maybe self-pay parking. There would be blind corners and empty sidewalks. It would be a thirty-something against a seventy-something. A blow from behind. A simple mugging. Happened all the time. How hard could it be?

The guy with the goatee jumped up and hustled down the aisle, following the guy with the money six feet behind.

Reacher got up and followed them both.

About the Authors

Karin Slaughter is one of the world's most popular and acclaimed storytellers. Published in 120 countries with more than 35 million copies sold across the globe, her nineteen novels include the Grant County and Will Trent books, as well as the Edgar-nominated *Cop Town* and the instant *New York Times* bestselling novels *Pretty Girls*, *The Good Daughter*, and *Pieces of Her*. Her most recent book, *The Last Widow*, features Sara Linton and Will Trent. Slaughter is the founder of the Save the Libraries project—a nonprofit organization established to support libraries and library programming. A native of Georgia, Karin Slaughter lives in Atlanta. Her standalone novels *Pieces of Her* and *The Good Daughter* are in development for film and television.

KarinSlaughter.com

Lee Child is one of the world's leading thriller writers. He was born in Coventry, raised in Birmingham, and now lives in New York. It is said one of his novels featuring his hero Jack Reacher is sold somewhere in the world every nine seconds. His books consistently achieve the number one slot on bestseller lists around the world, and have sold over one hundred million copies. Two blockbusting Jack Reacher movies have been made so far.

LeeChild.com